Jack the Ripper Victims Series
Apologies to the Cat's Meat Man

Alan M. Clark

More books in the Jack the Ripper Victims Series

Of Thimble and Threat
available in paperback, ebook, and audiobook

Say Anything but Your Prayer
available in paperback, and audiobook

A Brutal Chill in August
available in paperback, ebook, and audiobook

The Double Event
(comprised of the two novels *Of Thimble and Threat* and *Say Anything but Your Prayer*)
available in ebook, and audiobook

Each novel in the series is a standalone story.

Praise for the Jack the Ripper Victims Series

"*Of Thimble and Threat* is a terrifically absorbing read. A mature novel and superbly researched. The image of silver in the blood was woven expertly and made the ending luminous and poignant."

—Simon Clark, author of *Vampyrrhic* and *Night of the Triffids*

"Clark proves himself to be the ultimate double-threat, his prose every bit as evocative and compelling as his art. Steeped in Victoriana Say *Say Anything but Your Prayers* is a worthy edition to Ripperology."

—Steven Savile, author of *Silver* and *London Macabre*

"*A Brutal Chill in August*, one of a series wherein Alan M. Clark masterfully recreates the sorry lives of the Ripper's victims, is awash in atmospheric detail of those dark days in 19th century London. Exhaustively researched, Clark brings to life the plight of London's poor, and the extremes to which they must go in order to merely survive... or succumb as victims to disease, abuse, alcoholism, or worse. A great read."

—Elizabeth Engstrom, author of *Lizzie Borden* and *York's Moon*

The Double Event reviewed by Nancy Kilpatrick

Jack the Ripper stories invariably focus on the grisly murders and the mysterious identity of who-done-it. Jack's victims, desperate prostitutes in Whitechapel, London, are deemed pathetic creatures who, had they not been there working in the skin trade, wouldn't have been victims. In *Jack the Ripper Victim Series: The Double Event*, author Alan M. Clark guides readers away from those well-trod thought-paths to a clear, non-rosy window into the lives of two of the Ripper's victims, Elizabeth Stride and Catherine Eddowes, the 3rd and 4th respectively. We follow them from youth through adulthood. Forced by the values of a class-oriented Victorian society where legally women were chattel belonging to men, they made choices, none of which proves less evil than any other. These homeless, starving, devalued souls are victims of more than the Ripper's blade. Elizabeth and Catherine are real-life horror stories and, utilizing the tropes of fiction, Clark skillfully induces us to care about them from page one, even as they sink further into a future we know will ultimately lead to cruel death at the hands of a human monster. Clark's attention to details of the era reveals a class system where a poor woman alone is all but doomed to an early grave. Readers will come away touched by these profound portraits of desperate women and shocked by not just the crimes which ended in their demise, but the greater crimes of a society that offered them no hope. This book is a must-read; be prepared to be horrified.

—Nancy Kilpatrick, author of The Power of the Blood series, editor: *Danse Macabre* and *Expiration Date*

IFD Publishing
P.O. Box 40776, Eugene
Oregon 97404 U.S.A.
www.ifdpublishing.com

Copyright © 2017 by Alan M. Clark

All rights reserved. No part of this book may be reproduced or transmitted in any form or by any means, electronic or mechanical, including photocopying, recording, or by any information storage and retrieval system, without the written consent of the publisher, except where permitted by law.

This is a work of fiction. Although the novel is inspired by real historical events and actual human lives, the characters have been created for the sake of this story and are either products of the author's imagination or are used fictitiously. Any resemblance to actual events or locales or persons, living or dead, is entirely coincidental.

Cover art, Copyright © 2017 Alan M. Clark

Interior illustrations, Copyright © 2017 Alan M. Clark

ISBN: 978-0-9988466-1-3

Printed in the United States of America

Acknowledgments

Thanks to Melody Kees Clark, E. P. Clark, Dr. Frank Freemon, Cameron Pierce, Kirsten Alene Pierce, Eric M. Witchey, Elizabeth Engstrom, John McNichols, Laurie Ewing-McNichols, Michael Green, Jill Bauman, Ross E. Lockhart, Amanda Lloyd, Mike Covell, John Linwood Grant, David Bowles, Rodney Gardner, Paula Fye, Simon Clark, Mark Roland, Christine Morgan, and Lisa Snellings.

Special thanks to Stephen Vessels, my extra set of eyes on this novel.

For those willing to put themselves in another's shoes, no matter how ragged the footwear.

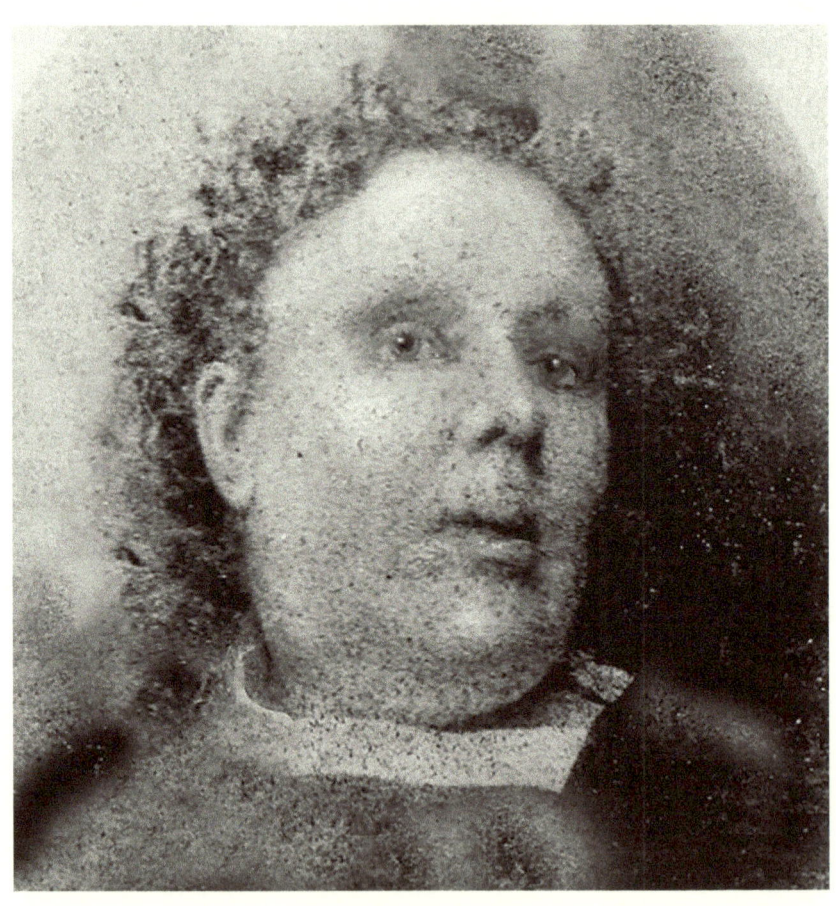
In an effort to bring life to and image of Annie Chapman, the author/illustrator manipulated a mortuary image of the woman to arrive at this portrait.

Author's Note—Historical Terror: Horror that Happened

In September 1888, after the brutal murders of Martha Tabram and Mary Ann "Polly" Nichols in August, how did Annie Chapman reasonably persuade herself to walk the streets of London's East End looking for a stranger to pay her for sex? Seeking an answer to that question was in part my purpose in writing *Apologies to the Cat's Meat Man*.

The novel is a work of fiction inspired by the life of Annie Chapman, a woman believed to be the second victim of Jack the Ripper. I made an effort to stick to what is known about her, yet for purposes of storytelling, I did not adhere strictly to her history, in part because much of her life is obscured by the relative anonymity she had in her time. I have assigned to my main character emotional characteristics and reactions that seem possible and consistent with her life and circumstances.

To be clear, the novel is not about Jack the Ripper. The Jack the Ripper Victims series, of which *Apologies to the Cat's Meat Man* is the fourth book, is not about the killer. Instead, each of its novels explores the life of a different victim. The books in the series can be read in any order, as each is a stand-alone account, their timelines overlapping.

For me, history is stories, perhaps more fact-based than fiction, but stories nonetheless. Good tales are driven by emotion. Following the emotional motivations of characters is compelling for me, as I think is true for most people. When the motivations are a mystery, such as those surrounding a horrible crime, I want to make sense of them. I want order in my world, and with horrible crimes, the acts by disturbed individuals and sometimes their victims hang out there in time, niggling for answers. Part of the puzzle that wants answering is context. How could that person do such a thing? What made their actions seem reasonable to them? Answers lie within the person's time and circumstances, the world as he or she knew it and how that individual in particular responded to the comforts and stresses within interpersonal relationships and environment.

History, sufficiently remote, but somewhat familiar, like the Victorian era, makes for interesting story context for me because I know something of that world. Remnants of that time still exist today, and I have communicated with family members who grew up close enough in time to the period that they knew something of the constraints and opportunities of life then. That era seems slightly alien and a little exotic. I also find I have a borrowed nostalgia for simpler times in which the people seemed to have had a naive innocence. Of course, that is a product of my complacency.

We're basically the same creatures we've been for thousands of years, with all the same emotions. What stimulates those emotions varies for all of us, yet we're good at interpreting and understanding others' moods within the context of their experiences.

When stories of times past hold situations sufficiently developed that the complexity of human emotion is revealed, that supposed innocence of a "simpler time" vanishes. Suddenly, understanding the historical and emotional context, the characters are no longer quaint and simple. I am right there with them, having some understanding of their motivations.

Through the research and writing of historical fiction novels, I must use my imagination to project myself into another place and time. In the midst of the effort, I feel like I'm engaged in time-travel. My wife often asks about that far off look in my eyes when I'm in the middle of a several-months-long project involving historical fiction. We might be at the grocery store or the post office at the time. Little does she know that I'm not actually standing next to her in those moments.

—Alan M. Clark
Eugene, Oregon

Jack the Ripper Victims Series
Apologies to the Cat's Meat Man

Alan M. Clark

Publishing
Eugene, Oregon

Rivals
Saturday, September 1, 1888

"You pay for Eliza's bed too," Annie said to Eddie, careful not to sound angry.

They sat together in the early evening at the Britannia Public House, known locally as the Ringers.

He gazed across the stained and worn table at her expressionless, his eyes cold and his mouth, hidden beneath his great mustache, offering no clue as to his feelings. Something about his look, a certain darkness around the eyes, echoed the frightful visage of Mr. Stewart, the cat's meat man Annie had feared when she'd been little. Whenever Annie had heard Mr. Stewart's song or seen him selling his tainted meat to pet owners about her childhood neighborhood, she'd fled and hidden from him.

What a pitiless master Eddie has become, Annie thought. *Too bad I can't say what I think of him.*

The day before, Francis Booth had told her of Eddie's two-timing with Eliza Cooper, and Annie had been trying to think of a way to talk to him about his deception.

Both Annie and Eliza lived at Crossingham's Lodging House in Dorset Street. Although an illegal practice, the lodging house deputy, Timothy Donovan, allowed Eddie to sleep with women on the premises. No doubt, whatever arrangement the two men had involved money.

Eddie was a brick layer's mate and pensioner with a curious surplus of funds. He currently had Annie over a barrel. She couldn't afford a room of her own without help. As he had done for the past few months, he'd paid half her lodging fee for the week at Crossingham's in exchange for sexual favors. Annie's room was held as long as she paid the rest, four pence, due each night. Failing to pay, she'd lose a night on the back end. If she missed paying three nights in a row, she'd lose the room.

Likely, he had the same arrangement with Eliza because, apparently, he spent other nights with her. He had been able to get away with his cheating because the women lodged in rooms on different floors, Annie in 29 on the second floor, and Eliza in 36 on the third floor.

Number 29 was small and drafty. The loose glass in the rotten window sash rattled when anyone mounted the lodging house stairs, and the floor creaked loudly beneath one's tread. The only heat available came through the open fanlight above the locked door to the adjoining room, number 28, which held the coal grate. Because the fanlight remained open, occupants in each room could hear what went on in the other.

On the good side, number 29 had a bed large enough for two. On the nights Eddie didn't spend with her, she had the straw mattress all to herself—quite a luxury.

At present, she had no other prospects for lodging without going to a doss house and sleeping with strangers.

With his silence, Eddie clearly indicated he didn't want to discuss the matter. In the midst of the busy pub, the hubbub of the patrons—the murmur of conversation, the laughter, the periodic shouting, the occasional insults hurled, both playful and serious—allowed him to turn away easily and ignore her as if he hadn't heard. To repeat herself would seem like harping.

"Drink your stout and I'll buy you another," Eddie said seductively.

Annie struggled to finish her drink without appearing to do so in a hurry. The stout felt warm and comfortable in her belly.

She picked up the copy of the Evening News Eddie had discarded on the table. In it, she found an article about the murder that had taken place two nights earlier. The story had been all over the streets since yesterday. A woman named Nichols had been brutally assaulted and murdered, her body left on the street less than a mile away.

"Did you read about the murder in Buck's-Row?" Annie asked Eddie. "Says her throat were cut, her bowel ripped open."

"Yes," he said. "I'm certain they've made it out to be much worse than it was." He waved his hand dismissively. "Another whore went against her minder."

Annie could easily believe that the newspapers, always in heavy competition with one another, exaggerated to make their stories more sensational and improve sales. What she'd heard on the street about the murder, coming through the rumor mill, was much the same. She set aside the paper.

"Although I paid on your room," Eddie said, "by chance, I may be gone much of the week. If so, you will give me extra satisfaction next week."

I hope you are gone this week, she thought, disgusted that he brought up their transaction in a public place. Becoming angry would do her no good. She tried to look relaxed, even as Eliza Cooper and Harry the Hawker came into the pub and approached the table.

"Sit," Eddie said, gesturing to empty seats, "and I'll buy you a drink."

The women merely nodded to one another.

"Dark Annie," Harry the Hawker said in greeting. He called her that, as many in the neighborhood did, because her dark hair helped distinguish her from Annie Platt, a woman with fair hair who also stayed at Crossingham's from time to time. Harry wore a brightly colored, green and coral-colored neckerchief, a ratty old maroon doublet, and a brown tricorn hat. His beard had grown exceedingly long and was held in an elaborate braid. "Anything to stand out in a crowd," he'd said to Annie one day. "That is the way to make a sale in a crowded market."

Eliza, a book seller, set down a heavy sack before taking her seat. She had a look of resentment about her as she looked at Annie. Possibly Francis had told Eliza about Eddie's two timing. Then again, she could be angry simply because Annie hadn't returned the soap she'd borrowed that morning.

Annie tried to relax and quiet her own resentment toward the woman while Eddie fetched drinks for everyone.

"Odd weather," Harry said. "Got cold early. Were a brutal chill in August too. Hard on my knees."

"Brutal, is it?" Eliza asked, chuckling. "Getting old, Harry?"

Harry merely huffed at her.

Annie could not determine Eliza's age. Her body seemed younger, more powerful than Annie's, but her round face had a weathered look. Her dark, curly hair had little gray.

Eddie returned, placed drinks before his guests and sat. He set a coin on the table, perhaps absentmindedly. Annie recognized the silver disk as a florin.

Eliza bent as if reaching for her sack, placing her right hand on the table for support, right atop the two shilling coin. When she straightened, holding a book, and lifted her hand, Annie saw that the two-shilling piece had become a penny.

"I've a new book to sell," Eliza said, holding up the volume, "*Strange Manuscript Found in a Copper Cylinder*, by James De Mille, what come all the way from New York City."

Seeing the theft, Annie thought she had an opportunity to turn Eddie against Eliza and have him all to herself.

Annie interrupted the woman's sales pitch, addressing Eddie. "She took your florin."

Eliza turned hateful eyes on her, as Eddie looked to the tabletop. He then looked at Eliza.

"Your sleeve might've thrown the coin to the floor," she said, her eyes wide, "so I moved it."

"You put a penny in its place," Annie said with disgust.

Eliza glared again, rose up, and swung a fist from across the table. The blow connected with the right side of Annie's face and bowled her over backwards out of her seat.

Harry the Hawker grabbed Eliza's shoulders and pulled her back. Nearby patrons of the pub paused to turned and watch the rough goings-on. Eliza got free, picked up her sack, and left the pub.

The slight lull in movement and sound within the establishment ended as Annie got up, righted her chair, and sat. She stared back at curious onlookers until most became uncomfortable and looked away.

She glanced at Eddie, hoping to see some evidence that he was displeased with Eliza. Instead, he gave Annie a stern look. He and Harry drank their stout, and said nothing about what had happened.

Exploring the tenderness around her right eye with her fingers, she winced in pain. The blow would leave a bruise.

Annie wanted to condemn Eliza's actions further, but couldn't afford to get on Eddie's bad side. Although ashamed of her opportunism, she couldn't help thinking bitterly, *That were an easy two shillings for Eliza.*

I must find a way to be done with Eddie. Once this week is past, I'll work harder to fully earn my nethers, so I don't depend on him.

Tenderness

In Annie's earliest memories, her family lived above the cobbler shop where her father, George Smith, worked in Harrow Road, Westbourne. The one room abode had a window facing south toward the road, a coal grate in the western wall, one bed, a table, three chairs, a small hutch, and an armoire. A doorway beside the fireplace gave access to a thin flight of stairs that ran crookedly around the chimney and down to the shop below.

The weathered building was of an older style, with its upper floor projecting out over the lower somewhat. The road in front remained busy with traffic, and all that came with being a broad thoroughfare. People passed by on horseback, in carriages, in wagons, or on foot, the sounds of their passing—the grind of wheels on cobblestones, the shouts of drivers, and the sounds of animals—continuous or intermittent, depending on the time of day. Those on foot sent up the soft sound of their tread, the murmur of their conversations, punctuated with laughter or angry words, and the occasional sounds of a scuffle or a fight. Above everything rose the barking of dogs, the whistles and horns of various steam-powered industries and conveyances, both of rail and the waterways, and the bells of churches and clocks.

Coal smoke from heating, cooking, and industry fouled the air along with the miasma of raw sewage from three main sources: the streets, privy vaults throughout the city, and the polluted River Thames. Scavengers gathered and sold to industry much of the solid raw sewage that dogs and horses dropped in the streets. Even so, the endlessly renewed supply of manure in the road and the easy access insects had to the privy vaults filled with human waste assured that flies bred in profusion. The insects got into everything.

The fluids of raw sewage remained on the street, and soaked in or eventually washed away with the rain, only to be replaced with more of the same. Periodically, when the ground had become saturated with liquid, the odor of horse urine, collected in puddles, became overwhelming. Privy vaults not emptied frequently enough overflowed at ground level during times of heavy rain. If the liquid waste couldn't make its way into the ground it slowly washed into the River Thames. The waterway reeked and had long been an unsafe place to wash clothes, bathe, or fish for food.

With all that, at the young age of five, Annie found herself overly sensitive and tender. The first time her mother, Ruth Smith, put her in a wool sweater, Annie panicked, feeling surrounded by itchiness. She cried with the pain and fright of the smallest cut to her skin.

The sight of bodily fluids and waste, particularly those belonging to others or animals, inspired her gorge to rise. Foul odors brought a gag at the least, and frequently took her last meal.

At night, shadows had a deepness that hid both cruel, mischievous beings and isolating pits of misery and loneliness. Even sleep held a fright, one inspired by the sight of a dead family member.

Annie had gone with her mother to attend a wake for a great aunt. Later in life, Annie would not remember the woman's name. The wake was the only time she ever saw her. The cold, gray look of the woman, as she rested on a table in the room where her family lodged, suggested to Annie a dreamless slumber.

From then on, nights with no dreams represented short periods of death. Without knowing which nights those might be, Annie saw all sleep as potentially a dark and perilous void. She resisted slumber.

After numerous restless nights following the great aunt's wake, Annie had become unhappy and ill-tempered from lack of rest. Her mother—Mum, she called her—didn't know what to do for her.

Annie's father—Dadda, she called him—sat beside her at bedtime one night. He looked at her with warm eyes, said simply, "Sleep," and gave her a delicate kiss on the forehead.

Annie fell asleep easily that night. Following that, without a goodnight kiss from her father at bedtime, she would not close her eyes.

At least a year would pass before Annie slept without the kiss first. Once the ritual had been broken, the goodnight kiss came only on the occasions Annie protested that she could not rest without it. Over time, the ritual occurred less frequently until the tender gesture was abandoned entirely.

The pain others experienced also aggravated Annie's tenderness. One day when she was perhaps seven years old, Dadda returned from his work unexpectedly while Annie busied herself, wringing laundry with the mangle. Mum had left her with the chore and gone to market, taking Annie's younger sister, Emily, with her.

Dadda showed her that his left index finger was broken. The digit, bruised and swollen, jutted away from the others at a sickening angle.

Annie struggle to hold down the bread and butter she'd eaten for breakfast.

Tall and proud, Dadda had a somewhat imposing manner despite his humble circumstances. He'd been in the 2nd Regiment of Life Guards, a cavalry regiment of the Royal family's household division that performed as bodyguards for the queen. He liked to think of himself as eminently capable and disciplined. Although his eyes could shine with warmth, they often turned cold suddenly. Dark hair, rarely tamed, topped his square head.

"Robert opened the gate on it whilst we unloaded a delivery," he said. "Were my fault. He had a customer, so I come to you for help."

Annie nodded uncertainly. Dadda sat at the table where they ate their meals, laid the hand palm up on the worn table top.

As she watched, astounded, he straightened and set the finger without shedding a tear. He took from his jacket pocket two short pieces of wood and three pieces of string, then placed the little boards, one below and one above the broken finger. "Tie the strings around the wood and fingers, Darling. Not too tight."

He grew impatient with her clumsy, trembling fingers, and used his good hand and his teeth to tighten the strings once she'd got them roughly placed.

"If you're to grow up, you'll want to harden yourself to such tasks, girl," he said.

Annie could tell she'd disappointed him. She could not imagine how adults endured the hardships of life, and wasn't at all certain she would survive into adulthood.

Dissembling
Monday, September 3

Annie had an egg to boil, one of two tiny brown ones, little bigger that a man's thumb, that she'd purchased at Spitalfields Market the day before. She carried it wrapped in her red and white neckerchief downstairs to the below-ground-level lodging house kitchen. Seeing Eliza there, Annie decided not to enter. With an uncomfortable mix of fear and anger, she thought about their encounter at the Ringers pub. Eliza was more pugnacious than Annie had anticipated. Worrying that she had started something she could not finish, her face became hot.

She removed her bonnet, tucked it into her brown bodice, and walked outside. Waiting for Eliza to leave the lodging house—as the woman seemed to do every morning around six o'clock—Annie stood out of the foot traffic beside the building, taking the air, watching the dawn light grow in the eastern sky, and considering the wretched neighborhood.

Increasingly, she felt trapped, pinned to the area by circumstance, much the way dead exotic insects she'd recently seen on display in a shop window had been held in place, skewered to a black background.

Dorset Street ran about 400 feet and was perhaps 25 feet wide, its pavement strewn with refuse, littered with paper, and liberally peppered with glass broken under foot, hoof, and wheel. If the rain didn't come to wash the street from time to time, the thoroughfare would have been mired in reeking filth and fluids.

During a time of high unemployment, with competition for jobs intensifying daily, at least a thousand poverty-stricken people occupied the low-cost, neglected housing that lined the streets. Given to vice, violence, and murder, the public houses in the neighborhood had reputations among the worst in London. The denizens and the law seemed to hardly notice the blood that frequently stained the footways, particularly in front of the pubs, before the gore turned brown, eventually blackened, and was forgotten.

Fully half those living in Dorset Street had "known life" since childhood, having grown up in families engaged in criminal activities of one form or another. Many though—men and women with debilitating injuries or dementia that left them physically or temperamentally incapable of competing for jobs—stayed because they could eke out an existence on less in Dorset Street. Others had fallen on hard times simply because they had no family support and did not contribute to a family's welfare. Employers considered middle-aged women—like Annie—who had lost their husbands, to be a poor risk. They preferred instead laborers with families and a home life because the responsibilities involved increased a worker's stability, readiness, and compliance. For the aging, single woman, temporary, low-wage work under harsh conditions might be found, but positions of employment had become rare.

Because of the inadequate employment opportunities, the poor in Dorset Street were easy prey for "family people," the criminal landlords of the lodging houses and the pubs of the area. Their scurfs and "demanders" often had only to threaten a nobbling or a visit from a "punisher" to persuade unfortunates to work for them as burglars, mug-hunters, dippers, and ladybirds. Most of the women found themselves under the thumbs of various whore minders or, like Annie, had unlawful arrangements with men.

The dangerous among the residents preyed upon whoever strayed into their territory with something of value. Annie remained safe in Dorset Street because she never had anything of significant worth. She and many others who lived there, just trying to get by, kept their heads down.

Having somewhat unusual skills in lace-making, Annie avoided working in the sweatshops most of the time. She made a meager income hawking on the streets her own lace and crocheted products, when she could afford the yarn and thread.

"Good morning!"

Annie let out a yelp, and cringed. Then she began to cough, a great racking that bent her over and hurt deep in her chest.

"Oh, dear," Amelia Palmer said, "and I was trying to have fun, sneaking up on you." The clatter of hooves and grind of wheels against the stones of the road had covered the sound of her approach. Amelia stood five and half feet tall, had dark hair, graying a bit, and a pale face with a long nose and weak chin. She stroked Annie's head of dark, wavy hair and patted her on the back to help soothe her. "I'm sorry I startled you."

Amelia had been a friend for several years. She also lived at Crossingham's. When the two women met, they had in common that they both lived apart from their husbands, yet received funds from them. To impress Amelia, Annie had given her to understand that her husband, John, actually a coachman, was instead a veterinary surgeon she'd once met in Windsor named Frederick Chapman.

Amelia's husband, Henry, had been a foreman at the docks, organizing lumpers through the Bosun's Pipe pub until an accident left him permanently injured. He received an Army Reserve pension of which he sent Amelia a portion. She had moved to the lodging house to be closer to the Jewish households she serviced as a charwoman.

After Annie's husband, John, died a year and a half past, the ten shillings he'd sent each week ceased to arrive. Although Amelia had no funds to offer, she'd been an ally in Annie's struggle to earn her keep.

Gaining control of herself, trying to ignore the painful pressure in her chest, Annie stood erect. Embarrassed, she casually waved away her friend's words of concern.

"How did you get the black eye?" Amelia asked.

"Eliza Cooper," Annie said. She glanced back at the entrance to Crossingham's, not wanting to miss seeing Eliza leave the establishment. "Do you know her? She hawks books, always has a sack of them."

"No, I don't know her."

"I were with Eddy when we saw Harry the Hawker and Eliza at the Ringers. We were having a fine time, and…for no reason, she got up and give me this."

Amelia made a face that suggested she thought there must be more to the story.

Annie shrugged. "So, he puts down a florin after buying drinks," she said. "Eliza palms the coin and leaves a penny in its place. I merely pointed out the theft."

Still unaccountably ashamed of her actions, Annie gave little sense of what had motivated her or Eliza.

As Amelia seemed about to question her account, Annie said quickly, "I'm feeling ill. I ought to go to my sister." To distract Amelia further, she brought up something from a previous discussion they'd had. "Should I get a pair of boots from her, I would go hop-picking." Amelia had been encouraging Annie to consider the migrant work available at farms in Kent as an additional means of earning. Annie had no intention of going to her sister, who considered her a nuisance, or going hop-picking.

She much preferred to earn money selling at Stratford Market products of her own making, but sales of her antimacassars and other lace and tatting goods suffered. Immigrants with clever hands continually undercut her. She had sold nearly all her products at a low rate, and needed to buy yarn before she could make more. A single antimacassar remained. Without begging, something she found herself unwilling to do, she'd had increasing difficulty paying her half of her lodgings and keeping herself fed.

Annie saw Eliza leave Crossingham's.

"Better than hopping," Amelia said, "the Green Dragon sweatshop is looking for fresh hands. You'll find it in Heneage Street."

That was good news. Annie had worked for sweaters before. Currently, she had no funds. If she could not sell the one antimacassar she had within the next few hours, she'd go looking for the place. "Do you have an address?"

"No, I just know where to go when I'm in the street," Amelia said. "Perhaps near Spelman. It's not hard to find."

Once they'd parted company, Annie went to the lodging house kitchen, fixed her tiny egg, and ate. She then retrieved the lone antimacassar from her room and headed for Stratford Market to try to make a sale.

A man who could have afforded her price of one shilling said, "I'll give you a tanner."

If she took his offer, she'd have four pence to pay up her lodgings, and two pence left over for the next day while she looked for work at the sweatshop. If she went hungry that night, and had her second egg in the morning, she'd get by.

Annie accepted the meager payment and handed over the beautiful lace product she'd spent much of a day creating.

Tossed coin

When Annie was little, Dadda had enjoyed surprising his girls with clever gifts that he made by hand. Presenting them as magical items added fanciful excitement to the events.

One afternoon when Annie was eight years old and Emily five, he told them, "I shall give you the gift of a bird in a cage." He produced a white rectangular card, drew a bird on one side, a cage on the other. He punched two small holes in the card along each of two opposing sides. He passed a piece of string through each of the holes and tied it in place. Then, turning the card over and over, he wound up the strings. As he pulled on them with his hands, the card spun around swiftly. The bird seemed to appear inside the cage, delighting both girls. He taught Annie how to make the toy work so she could put the bird in the cage.

"That's a thaumatrope," he said, kissing his girls on their heads. "Now, go show your friends."

Annie and Emily proudly shared their new toy with others. Annie told her friends what a wonderful father she had. She loved him dearly.

As time passed, Annie noticed that his mood darkened occasionally, especially when he smelled of drink. Although increasingly grouchy over time, he continued to show that he loved his girls with an occasional kind word and the unusual gifts. He made them whistles from empty thread spools. He made paper fish that, given a drop of oil, would swim across a wash tub as if alive. He crafted carriages, ships, and little houses from empty match boxes.

By the time Annie reached the age of ten, he seemed to smell of drink most of the time. She continued to love her clever father, yet he wasn't the same.

On a good day, one in which he'd had little to drink, he told Annie, "You are my favorite. Being the first, you can't help it. You're the clever one, and you have a good heart. When you're grown and the young men come for you, I'll be jealous, I will. But I'll let you have your way, as a good father should do."

A good thing Emily didn't hear him say that, Annie decided, although she wondered if he might have said the same to her sister.

Other times, while deep in his cups, George Smith was as mean as ever a man could be. He'd twist Annie's ears just to hear her squeal so he could call her "little piggy." She learned to keep her eyes on his feet and hands to anticipate his blows, none of them for discipline—he left that to Mum—and not hard, though painful enough to get her attention. Frequently, Annie had to dodge his feet as he tried to step on her toes. "I must teach you to dance," he'd say, and laugh.

Feeling betrayed by Dadda's mean-spirited behavior, she told herself that her overly sensitive nature whinged unnecessarily.

When she turned eleven, he said, "Better you should work than go to school, girl. You must do your part."

"She'll stay in school," Mum said.

"Then she'll be doing piece work, making match boxes and applying labels at night," he said.

"No, she won't," Mum said flatly. "She'll rest in the evening and devote her days to education so she'll be intelligent enough to avoid marrying the likes of you."

Neither fat nor thin, short nor tall, Ruth Smith looked steady and confident. Her brown eyes rarely appeared troubled. She kept her dark hair confined. Unlike her husband, she didn't seem to have a fanciful bone in her body, but she knew how to get on with whatever George Smith brought to her life, and she did so without complaint.

Strangely, as if they had a pact between them, Mum never said anything about Dadda's drinking, and he never took exception to her harsh words.

Mum got her way concerning Annie's education. That didn't stop Dadda from resenting his eldest daughter for not contributing to the household income.

He took to criticizing and calling her names. He mocked Annie's efforts in school, her reading, and attempts to engage in adult conversation, telling her that she was too immature to understand much of anything. "It'll be a wonder if you live to become grown," he said once.

After one of his cruel tirades, Emily found Annie sitting on the rotting steps that led down to the cobbler shop.

"Why are you *crying?*" Emily asked. She mocked her sister, making a pouting face and pantomiming fists against her eyes.

"Dadda calls me names," Annie said. "He says I'm ugly, foolish, and dimwitted."

"You're his *favorite*," Emily said with a sneer.

Possibly she'd heard him say that and didn't like being the lesser.

Annie certainly didn't feel favored. "He doesn't call *you* names." she said.

"A little. Not as much as you." Emily made another face and stuck her tongue out. "You can be the favorite. I shan't want it."

Periodically, but with increasing rarity, Dadda did emerge from drunkenness to show a bit of love.

"His heart has two sides, the good and the bad," mum would say. "Like a tossed coin what doesn't like to land on its edge, and one side cannot see the other."

With time, Annie came to understand the connection between her father's cruelty and drink. When sober and his good side came to the fore, he became sweet to his children to make up for the times he'd treated them badly. He couldn't admit to his bad behavior, remained too proud to apologize, and his efforts to compensate seemed awkward and not heart-felt.

Fight
Tuesday, September 4

About five o'clock Tuesday morning, Annie stepped into the lodging house deputy's office. Good morning, Tim," she said.

"Good morning, Dark Annie. Come to pay up?"

"Yes." She offered the big man the tanner she'd earned selling her last antimacassar. "Just for tonight. I'll need the remainder."

Waiting for him to unlock his money drawer, she wondered about Eddie. He hadn't come to her room last night. She hoped he had indeed gone away for the week.

Mr. Donovan offered Annie two pennies.

"Thank you," she said, and left his office.

Annie took her second egg down to the kitchen, poached it, and ate while talking with the other lodgers seated at the kitchen tables, mostly middle-aged and older women. Directly across the table from her sat withered and white-haired Pearl Watkins. She'd had at least one egg for her breakfast, much of the food evident on her face and hands. At least ninety years old, much escaped Pearl's notice.

On the old woman's left sat Louisa McGregor, a great blocky woman with fair hair and skin, who might have been mistaken for a man if dressed differently.

To her right sat dark-eyed, olive-skinned Alice Lacroix. She usually ate what Pearl left behind during a meal.

"Good morning, Dark Annie," Alice said, her French accent always a pretty thing to hear.

"Good morning," Annie said.

Louisa nodded.

"Ain't we lucky to have rooms up high?" Pearl said.

Annie assumed she meant rooms above ground level since all four had second floor lodgings. Sometimes the old woman said things that didn't make sense.

Eliza entered, set about preparing a cup of coffee, and sat eating bread and cheese at the other table. Annie avoided looking in her direction.

"My sister, Agatha," Pearl said, "what lives with me here when she's got the chink, she says the blue bottles are keeping people awake at night."

"We know Agatha," Louisa said in a tired voice.

"How do they do that," Annie asked.

Pearl shrugged. "Loud noises?"

Louisa shook her head. "They're not awakening everyone. Agatha often sleeps rough."

"Not my fault," Pearl said. She looked around the table uneasily.

"Just those on the street," Alice said, kindly patting Pearl's gnarled hand as it lay upon the table, smeared with yellow yolk. "They don't use loud noises." Alice clearly tried to show how patient she could be. "The constables are enforcing the old Vagrancy Act against sleeping rough. They want to make the streets safer after the killing of that poor woman in Buck's-Row." Alice put her fingers to her mouth and licked off the yolk she'd lifted from the old woman's hand. Again, appearing companionable, she placed her hand back atop Pearl's, then licked her fingers once more.

Agatha was at least eighty years old, and in greater possession of her faculties than her sister, Pearl. She had frightened Annie with stories about the dangers of the night. She also gave Annie the rules of sleeping rough in case she ever needed them. "You never know what might befall," Agatha had said ominously.

Still trying to piece together the parts of the conversation, Annie asked, "The constables wake those sleeping rough and keep them from sleeping?"

"Yes," Alice said. "Should they see you with eyes closed, they rouse you and make you move on. They know all the best sleeping spots and clear the homeless out of them."

"Poor Agatha hasn't had any sleep since Friday night," Pearl said.

Annie didn't know which was worse: sleeping amidst the hazards of the night or exposure to the dangers combined with no rest. "Yes, we are lucky," she agreed.

Pearl gave her a sloppy, yellow smile.

Finished with her egg and conversation, Annie stood in the queue of those waiting to wash their dishes. Eliza appeared right behind her, giving her glaring looks. Annie tried not to let on that the intimidation got to her. When her turn came, she washed with a greasy rag and a sliver of soap so small that it completely dissolved in the gray water as she scrubbed. Her bowl and spoon were all that remained of the set she and her husband, John, had bought shortly after their wedding. She didn't feel good about leaving them dirty.

The majority of the lodgers had left the kitchen. As she stood drying her bowl and utensil, Eliza, next in the queue to use the basin, turned on her. "That were my soap you used up," she said, "and now I don't have any. Thief!"

"The pot calling the kettle black," Annie said. She reached into her pocket, pulled out a coin, and threw it on the closest table. "Here's a ha'penny. Go get some more soap."

Those still in the kitchen, hurried out, Pearl hobbling up the stairs last.

"You steal more than soap," Eliza growled quietly. "Francis told me about you and Eddie."

By the woman's tone and the wild look in her eyes, Annie knew she faced trouble. She tried to exit the kitchen, but Eliza grabbed her, hooked a foot around Annie's left leg, and threw her to the floor. Eliza fell upon her, and began beating her with fists.

Annie returned the blows as best she could, landing a solid one to the woman's face. Blood flowed from Eliza's lip. Yet, while Annie cried out in pain and flinched away when struck, Eliza seemed to absorb the punishment without reaction. Her steady expression suggested she was impervious to pain. Frightened, Annie gave up, covered her head with her arms, and waited for the blows to cease.

Finally, gulping for breath, Eliza seemed to tire. She wrestled Annie into a supine position, knelt on her hip, and leaned over her. "Leave Crossingham's," she said, thrusting her face, jaw first, toward Annie's, and looking down her nose. "Should I see you here again, I'll give you worse."

When a girl, the one time Annie had been surprised by the cat's meat man, she'd bumped into him as he came around the corner of the building where she lived. He'd looked down on her in the same manner.

Looking at Eliza, Annie felt herself shrinking inside. She briefly became a gibbering child. "No, I'll go—I didn't—I haven't had—should never have…"

"Get up and get out," shouted the night watchman, John Evans, as he entered the room. "I'll not have fights in my kitchen. Mr. Donovan will be here any moment, and you know he'll be much harder than I am."

Eliza backed off, took the ha'penny from the table, and left.

Annie got up, went toward the stairs, then hesitated.

Evans, or Brummy, as folks called him, looked at Annie with green eyes narrowed. He was a sturdy fellow with dark hair in a terrier crop. His large hands rose from his sides, palms up. "What are you waiting for?"

"I don't want to meet Eliza on the stairs."

Evans shook his head in disgust, and went up, taking the treads two at a time.

Shamed, Annie followed. On the ground floor, instead of going up to her room, she fled the lodging house into the dawn, not knowing what else to do. She moved eastward along Dorset Street, fearing that Eliza would come after her again if she stayed at Crossingham's.

Through the dimness, Annie saw Amelia Palmer emerge from the public urinals across Commercial Street near Christ Church. Needing to see a friendly face and not wanting to be alone in case Eliza came for her, she lifted her skirts slightly, and hurried to cross the road. The traffic along Commercial Street was heavy that time of day. Annie threaded a route between a van, a couple of traps, and a traveling carriage, all stalled as they waited for the crossing at Fournier and Brushfield Streets to clear. She encountered "mud" of various depths as she went, fouling her boots nearly to her instep.

"Amelia," she called out as she mounted the footway on the other side.

Her friend, headed toward Fournier Street, stopped, turned, and smiled as Annie approached. "You look worse today," Amelia said, "very pale, and your bruise is even bigger."

With the opportunity to show righteous indignation to a sympathetic friend, Annie regained some of her courage. "Look at my chest." She opened her black coat and two bodices enough for Amelia to see the large red bruises on her breast. "Eliza did that just now after accusing me of stealing soap. She's gone mad."

Again, Annie didn't tell her friend the full story.

When Amelia looked as if she might ask questions about the fight, Annie interrupted.

"I'll want to earn at least two pence, ha'penny today if I want to stay in my room tonight. Eliza is bent on keeping me out, so I might stay elsewhere for a bit. I can afford to not pay up at Crossingham's for two more days. Should I miss the third one, I'll lose the room. Will you retrieve my lace-making accoutrements, and whatever other supplies you find and put them in your room?" Annie offered her key.

"Yes," Amelia said. "When shall I see you to return this?"

"Perhaps tonight."

"How about the hopping?" Amelia asked. "You don't need a room whilst you pick hops. There are shacks for the workers. And you can get away from the mad woman."

Annie knew she could sign up and get aboard one of the many wagon-loads of paupers headed for Kent, but she didn't want to travel to the countryside with almost no money in her pocket. "Still no boots."

"Did you try for work at the sweatshop?"

"That's what I'm about right now," Annie told her. "Will you show me where it is?"

"I have errands. You'll find it. Look for the red sign, says 'Green Dragon Shirting and Trouser.'"

Annie nodded.

Amelia considered her for a moment. "You need something to help you feel better. Take this and buy tea, not drink." She offered two pence.

"Thank you," Annie said. Now she needed a mere ha'penny to have enough to pay up her room for the night.

"You've got to find work," her friend said with a concerned look, and walked away, disappearing among the foot traffic.

As Annie headed toward Heneage Street, she imagined the Green Dragon would be as miserable a place to work as any other sweatshop, a stuffy room crowded with miserable workers who had to provide their own trimmings—thread, buttons, and perhaps certain types of cloth. The sweater would be brutal in his or her effort to drive the laborers to meet quotas.

The last time Annie had done such work, she'd finished waistcoats for a sweater in Poplar. When she arrived the first day, she'd had to work for two hours to pay for the purple shell buttons and the specific plum-colored thread required for the job and furnished by the sweater.

At present, Annie carried with her white, blue, black, brown, green, and red thread. The only money she had was the two pence Amelia had given, and one pence, ha'penny left over from yesterday's sale of the antimacassar. If the sweater she sought had other requirements, and demanded payment for the supplies before her labor commenced, Annie might not have the price needed to secure the work.

What I need to face the labor and the sweater is to be fortified. I could spend Amelia's two pence on a half-quartern of rum.

If she did that, she'd certainly risk arriving at the sweater with too little funds.

I shouldn't have to pay to gain employment, she thought defiantly.

Annie imagined her sweet husband scolding her gently. She remembered his words on the occasions she had preferred to drink her breakfast. "You've got to eat, my dear, to keep your girlish figure." When he said "girlish figure," he'd always meant what he called her generous dairy and plump backside.

Not quite so plump now, she thought, and wagged her backside slightly as she walked.

Plump enough, John seemed to say.

Annie pictured her husband looking at her as he often had with an exaggerated lascivious look. She chuckled in spite of herself. John had always been able to get a laugh out of her, even if she was distressed and unhappy.

Although he'd been dead and gone for at least a year and a half, his words seemed to enter her thoughts from time to time. Annie liked to think he watched her, a desiring look in his eyes and a wry comment ready on his lips. She remembered his face and his boyish smile as he chided her playfully or gave good advice. With life increasingly difficult since his death, Annie welcomed the fanciful presence. Her beloved John had been nothing if not a good companion. He'd been a drunk, like Dadda, but without the dark side.

Annie stepped into the Black Eagle pub in Brick Lane and had her rum.

Cat's Meat

Around age twelve, Annie cut her right hand while helping her mother slice bread for an evening meal. Over the ensuing muggy summer days, the wound became red and hot. The hand swelled and the wound began to suppurate.

Early evening of one of those days, when their room above the cobbler shop had grown unbearably stuffy, she lay miserable and wet from sweat in bed, trying to ignore the throbbing pain in her right hand, and an increasing need to get up and use the chamber pot.

"You must get better so we can play Old Maid," Emily seemed to say to the doll cradled in her lap, though clearly she meant the words for Annie. The two sisters didn't get along most of the time, possibly because Emily knew Dadda looked upon Annie as his favorite. Still, she sat in a chair beside the bed and held Annie's left hand. "I'm no good alone, and Mum's too busy to play."

Their father came clomping up the stairs. Annie heard him hop over the two rotten treads beneath the roof leak and the room shook a bit. She ceased to moan and writhe for fear of disappointing him. Mum, preparing supper, greeted Dadda, then he moved to the bed to have a look at Annie. Over top the odors of old leather and shoe black, he smelled most strongly of drink.

"If it worsens," he said, turning toward Mum, "she'll lose the hand."

"No, Dadda!" Annie cried as he turned back to her.

Emily made a face and climbed down from the chair. She dropped the doll as she backed away toward Mum.

Hot tears poured from Annie's eyes. She shifted uncomfortably in the bed and the rough straw inside the mattress bit into her painfully. Her bladder let go and she urinated there in the bed. He would discover the urine later, but she could not worry about that yet.

"Should they take your hand," Dadda said, "they'll give it to the cat's meat man. You don't want that, do you?"

Emily buried her face in her mother's skirts.

"He's teasing you," Mum said. "Don't believe your father."

Busy, her defense of her daughter was weak and did not prevent the girl's imagination from providing further torment. Annie saw the cat's meat man, Mr Stewart, in his broad, brightly colored neckerchief, selling her severed fingers, dyed green and stabbed onto wooden skewers, to Mrs. Salter, who lived in the building next door. The woman kept a dog and a cat, and bought meat regularly from Mr. Stewart to feed her animals.

Thinking that one hand might satisfy the takers as well as the other, Annie frantically tried to pull herself together enough to say, "Tell them to take the other one, Dadda. It doesn't work as well." Sobs came out instead, drowning in the salty fluids of her mouth and nose.

"Cease your blubbering, girl," Dadda said. "I'm trying to make you fight for that hand. We would not give it to the cat's meat man." Then he smiled with mischief. "Yet if you don't fight to keep it, he may come in the night for it all the same. I'll leave the padlock off the door to make it easier."

"You are a drunken lout, George Smith," Mum said, "terrorizing your own young the way you do." She threw a wooden spoon. The implement smacked into Dadda's head with a loud knock and bounced off. Unfazed, his mischievous smile remained.

Too late, Mum moved to settle Annie's fears and calm her.

Although the wound healed and she kept her hand, afterward she knew she wasn't up to the hardships life would throw at her. As she grew, Annie found her squeamish and fearful response to the world an increasing source of distress. She would have to become someone else if she wanted to survive.

The cat's meat man seemed to follow her around and pop up in her imagination when Annie felt vulnerable.

Pavement

By noon, Annie had been up and down the short length of Heneage Street several times looking for the Green Dragon sweatshop without success. Her back, hips, and feet ached as she moved along the unyielding granite cobblestones.

Because she trusted Amelia Palmer, she knew the sweatshop must exist. Annie decided she'd have to ask someone for directions. Oddly, as she considered approaching a stranger, she thought of her father. As with approaching a stranger, she'd never known what she would get from Dadda; a heart of goodwill or one of angry mischief. Although she loved him, because of his drinking, he might have presented either of those.

As she thought about speaking to a man sweeping blackness out of a doorway, she considered her appearance. She had not afforded herself a bath lately, nor washed her clothes. Her clothing was hopelessly threadbare; her cuffs, collars, and hems frayed, stained, and wilted. She had the black eye that Eliza Cooper had given her. The injury had been purple and blue on Sunday when she'd looked in a mirror. At present, the bruise probably appeared green and yellow.

At least most of the evidence of her fight over soap remained hidden under her clothes.

Yes, you look and perhaps smell the muck snipe, but there isn't anything for it.

Finally, Annie swallowed, took a deep breath and approached the man sweeping out the doorway. As he caught sight of her, he winced and leaned on his worn broom. Unabashed, he looked her up and down critically as she spoke.

"I'm looking for a sweater in Heneage Street."

His mouth and nose twisted in an expression of scorn.

He doesn't know you, John seemed to say. Annie was grateful for the effort to save her feelings.

I would not be quite this wretched if not for Eliza.

"Can't say I've heard of it," the man said, turning away, "I don't rent to sweaters." He went on with his sweeping.

Annie choked on the cloud he sent up, backed away, and stumbled on. Thankfully, the breeze took most of the dust away from her. Still, she coughed uncontrollably into her hands until dizziness compelled her to lean against the brick wall of the tenement. When the hot coughing fit had ended, she noticed a spot of blood in her left hand.

My gums bleed again, she told herself to forestall much worse thoughts about her health.

"Don't think you can fetch up against my building," the man called out. He started toward her. "Go on, now."

Annie bent her aching back forward, shuffled her sore feet, one in front of the other on the worn pavers, and he faded slowly into the distance.

She made another circuit of Heneage Street. In broad daylight, the sweatshop should be obvious. "Look for the red sign, says 'Green Dragon Shirting and Trouser,'" Amelia had said.

Or had she said a green sign with a picture of a red dragon on it?

~ ~ ~

Annie bought a cup of eel jelly from a street vendor passing through Heneage Street on his way to Commercial Street.

"I shan't turn down a ha'penny," he said as he ladle up her cup, "but I haven't the time to watch you eat."

She stood with her spoon and cup beside the vendor's cart, eating the slimy stew at a reasonable pace. Possibly having expected her to gulp the food down, he grumbled for a time and made angry eyes at her, then set about with other small preparations for his day of sales that he no doubt would have saved until he got to Commercial Street.

Defying the man, Annie gained a bit of courage. She imagined facing Eliza at Crossingham's and striking her down with a single great blow to the crown of her head. Annie had rarely fought in her life, and assumed that if she were fast, she would succeed. She was certainly angry enough.

A thief, Eliza will take my man, given the chance. She found the thought that she continued to claim such a cold-hearted fellow as her own unsettling, considering what it cost her. What Eddie's coin bought had never truly been sufficient recompense for what she lost in dignity.

Finally, she returned the vendor's cup and spoon. He gave her a resentful look, and they both moved off in opposite directions.

~ ~ ~

Annie saw Eliza enter the street walking in the opposite direction, carrying her sack of books.

In a city of millions, I should easily avoid her!

As Annie turned and fled toward an opening between two buildings and ducked inside, she remembered her thoughts of attacking the woman. She imagined Eliza wielding her heavy sack like a weapon, and the pain of hard, sharp book corners striking soft flesh. Annie hid behind a cluster of dust bins.

Eliza walked by on the footway just beyond the opening to the street.

Hatred awoke in Annie as she watched the woman's confident stride. Something about the gait recalled Dadda's, when in his cups. Annie saw a splintery, broken shovel handle, about three feet in length, and decided that would give her the advantage she needed over the woman. She would give Eliza a beating that would teach her a lesson.

Swiftly and quietly, Annie crept out of the opening and caught up with her. She raised the handle high, thinking about bringing the oak shaft down on her father's head.

No, she could not hurt *either* of them!

Annie shrank away from her actions at the last moment and choked on her anger. She commenced to cough, dropped the broken handle, and fell to the footway as Eliza turned around. Holding her chest, Annie writhed on the worn flagstones, her throat and lungs hacking away despite her efforts to stop.

The glimpses of Eliza's face displayed a complex reaction, as her surprised features grew angry, shifted to a look of contempt or amusement, then settled on a touch of pity and even fright before she turned away and walked on, shaking her head.

Annie didn't know what to make of the woman's response.

Once her coughing fit finally quieted, she felt incapable of asking for work, let alone doing any. Knowing she had little time left to earn what she needed to pay up her room, she headed for the Whitechapel Workhouse.

With my bruises, they might give me a bed in the Union Infirmary. With a good night's rest, I'll be ready to find work tomorrow. I'll pay up at Crossingham's and get back into number 29, whether Eliza likes it or not.

Missing Treads

When she was fifteen years old, Annie and her sister, Emily, witnessed the birth of their sister, Georgina. On that day, their father had traveled south of the river to help Mum's father, also a cobbler. Mum endured the pain of childbirth with little vocal complaint as she lay in bed in their tiny room above the cobbler shop.

Having found work in the last few years at a cotton spinning mill and a laundry, Annie led a much less protected life than when younger and had gained a somewhat tougher hide regarding the grotesque. She remained tender, though, especially in reaction to expressions of pain, like those on her mother's face. As the hours of Mum's labor stretched on, they quickly grew unbearable.

Every chance she got, Annie retreated to the stairs that led from their room to the cobbler shop below. She sat halfway down the crooked flight on a tread above a hole where Dadda had removed two treads that had rotted away beneath a roof leak. He'd promised to replace the treads even as he'd torn them out two years earlier. Ever since, the family had all been using the thin middle tread support Dadda called the stringer. A wonder that none of them had suffered a fall, especially Mum, as difficult as it had been lately for her to see her feet.

Dangling her feet and legs through the hole, Annie gazed into the closed shop below. She tried to watch the changing light coming through the front windows move across the shop floor. If the light moved, time was passing and the dreadful day would eventually end.

But for the shadows of a few birds in flight, the brightness spitefully would not budge.

Mum's expressions of pain reminded Annie of an accident she'd witnessed near her work station at the cotton spinning mill. A handsome, young fettler, working on a dangerous part of the mechanism still in motion, had lost to the machine two fingers from his right hand so suddenly he had only a troubled look to see the digits lying upon the down-strewn floor. He displayed no sign of pain until some time had passed, had even bent to pick a finger up and try to fit it back in place. Somehow, that lack of initial reaction made his response worse when it did come, with a wide-eyed grimace of gape-mouthed horror; with gasps, moans, and shrieks of pain.

Annie had cut herself with knives so sharp, she hadn't felt the injuries at first. She imagined the cat's meat man having knives and shears that sharp, and that she might not know he'd taken from her until he'd got away with it.

Annie's mother displayed reactions similar to those of the young fettler. Knowing something of sex, she thought, *Dadda stabbed Mum months ago, and its taken this long for her to feel it.*

All too ugly and frightening to think about, Annie felt a rising panic. She pushed the thoughts away and concentrated again on discerning the movement of the light in the cobbler shop below.

Emily came to her periodically for help. At great emotional cost, Annie moved to help each time, then looked for a lull in activity to retreat to the stairway again.

Upon return after attending to her mother's needs, she saw that the light had indeed moved below. Despite understanding the process of the Sun's seemingly slow procession across the sky, Annie got the impression that when she selfishly hid from her duty to her mother, the passage of time became ponderous and stubbornly slow to punish her.

"You must stop being a baby and help," Emily said the third time she came to retrieve Annie, "or I'll tell Dadda."

Annie didn't want to give her father more fodder for criticism. She gave up the stairway and sat with Emily and her Mother. Annie hoped for a distraction of daydreams. Instead she spent her time quietly weeping and trying unsuccessfully to not think of the pain Mum endured. Emily, shaking her head and muttering under her breath, watched Annie with barely disguised loathing.

As the baby came, the blood and gore horrified Annie. Emily helped Mum while Annie cringed in a corner, retching into a basin. With no meal served that day because of her mother's labor, nothing emerged but a hot and sour clear liquid that further sickened her.

Annie cried more than her mother did that day.

That night, as she lay in bed trying to sleep with her family, she wasn't certain she wished to survive into adulthood. Emily, lying between her older sister and their parents, was pure boney resentment, all elbows and cold shoulders whenever Annie tried to cuddle up close. Annie wanted a kiss from her father to help her go to sleep, but she'd missed her chance, and at her age, she would have felt foolish asking for the tender gesture, anyway.

Two years later, when their sister, Mirium, was born, Dadda stepped out to get drunk as Mum's labor began. Annie stuck with Emily, and got a couple of smiles for her effort.

Later, after the child had come and Dadda returned home, Emily complained, "You left us just when we needed you most."

"You could have helped," Annie said. "We're not midwives."

"You two did well enough with Georgina, " he said. "I thought I'd be in the way."

Whitechapel Workhouse

Annie joined a queue that wound through the courtyard outside the Union Infirmary before entering the door to the receiving offices. As she waited with the countless others applying for admittance to the workhouse infirmary, a woman wrapped in a blanket and sitting in a decrepit bath chair spoke to her.

"Name's Silvy," she said.

"Annie."

"You don't stand much of a chance of getting in," Silvy said. Both of her lower legs were missing. She had labored breathing. Earlier, when she'd lifted her blanket to adjust her partial limbs, Annie had seen that the woman had purple sores on her thighs from sitting in the contraption too long. "They don't have enough medical people, so they send whatever staff they have to size up the applicants. Even with the bruises, you don't look ill."

Others, a man with a large gash in his forehead, and a woman in the beginning stages of child labor, nodded their heads in agreement.

What business is it of theirs? Annie wondered, then realized that the great number of those applying for relief hurt the chances of the truly needy getting in. *I can hardly blame them for wanting to discourage me, yet I need help too.*

Silvy pointed out a man further up the queue. The fellow was about thirty years old. Aside from his raggedy clothing he looked to be in good shape. "He joined the queue after telling us the casual ward is full. His cause is hopeless."

The queue moved at a snail's pace. Silvy periodically asked Annie for help moving forward. She'd gripped the handle at the rear of the conveyance and pushed, glad to feel useful. As the wait outside the receiving offices seemed interminable, Annie wavered between remaining in the queue, and taking her chances with the night.

A young man with a bag over his shoulder came out of the building's large front doors and made his way along the line of paupers assembled in the courtyard, speaking with them one at a time. Occasionally, he reached into his bag and offered a person a small object, then gestured toward the street. Sometimes, the person he spoke to seemed to argue with him, but all of those eventually left the queue and headed for the street. Annie decided to wait to see what he had to offer.

The woman in labor lost her water and sat on the gritty pavement. Annie tried to help support her back to keep her from falling all the way to the hard damp flagstones. The woman cried out, and others in the queue drew the attention of the young man to the pregnant woman. He disappeared inside for a moment and returned with a nurse. After the nurse performed a brief examination, she and the young man helped the pregnant woman up, and led her slowly and awkwardly inside.

Silvy turned to Annie. "Plenty as comes to the infirmary looking knapped merely want a bed."

The young man took up his brief interviews again. Finally, having passed over those obviously ill, he stopped before Annie. "And your complaint?"

"I have dizzying coughing spells, terrible faintness, and pains all over from a fight." She presented her bruises, pulling her jacket and bodices apart enough for him to see her shoulder, and pointing to the more obvious injury around her right eye.

He seemed a bit shocked and irritated that she'd expose herself like that. Annie had long since disposed of such trivial modesty.

"Take these for your cough," he said, reaching into his bag, and offering her a small box. "Your bruises will heal on their own. Perhaps you should not fight." He gestured toward the street.

His voice told of his middle class station and that he'd been educated somewhat. Annie thought he might be a volunteer. Although probably a good man, he presumed to offer advice without knowledge of her circumstances or her role in what had transpired. Annie wanted to forgive him the cold statement, despite her resentment.

The container he'd given her functioned like a matchbox, with a small drawer that slid out to give access to the interior. About ten small white tablets rested inside.

"What are they?" she asked. She had a bottle of pills in her room from an earlier visit concerning her cough. On that occasion, a nurse she met told her she had influenza, had given her the medicine, and sent her away. She'd stopped taking the pills because they didn't seem to help, and upset her stomach. What the young man had given her looked different.

"Pills," he said impatiently, yet with some hesitation.

"What do they do?"

He looked embarrassed, but his features rallied with a slight smugness "I'm told to give them to those with a cough," he said. "I should think it's good advice."

He's uncomfortable because he doesn't know what he's doing. Her resentment had turned to sympathy.

Annie left the Union Infirmary fearing a night sleeping rough.

She remembered that while at the Ringers on Saturday, she'd read in the Evening News about the Nichols murder that occurred Thursday night/Friday morning. The brutal mutilation and killing had taken place not far from where Annie currently stood. She remembered that in early August, another woman had been killed in George Yard, stabbed at least thirty times.

When asked if he knew of the Nichols murder, Eddie had said, "Yes. I'm certain the Evening News made it out to be much worse than it was. Another whore went against her minder."

At the time, she'd easily believed that. At present, as she considered a night on the streets, she *needed* to believe what he'd suggested. *In a city of millions, the odds are against running into a murderer. And if I sleep rough, I'll be able to look for work starting early in the morning.*

She remembered from her earlier conversation with Alice, Pearl, and Louisa about the police enforcing the old Vagrancy Act that forbid sleeping rough. Although that might increase the safety on the streets, she'd likely get little rest.

Annie heard cursing and a struggle down Thomas Street toward the entrance to the workhouse casual ward. She waited and watched as two young women came walking toward her.

"Thieving, is it?" one of them said in a mocking tone, "Who in the casual ward has anything to prig."

Annie assumed the women had been turned out in the street, which would leave a couple of openings for admittance to the casual ward. She wavered again, knowing she had to make a decision quickly before others seeking relief found out and took her place.

If she entered the casual ward, she'd be required to stay for two nights, and she'd owe them a day's work, probably picking oakum. She didn't want to do that, but she'd done the work before and survived. She would miss paying up her lodgings for the two nights and her opportunity to earn enough to pay up on the third night, the one she could not miss without losing the room, would be greatly diminished. Yet staying away from Crossingham's for two nights might give Eliza's anger a chance to cool. As unhappy as Annie was about her choices, most of all, she feared a night on the streets.

She hurried to the entrance and pounded on the door beneath the high stone arch. "Let me in," she shouted, and pounded again.

I'll give them a false name and try to escape tomorrow.

Finally, a burley fellow dressed in a black and gray uniform answered the door.

"You're in luck, old girl," He said, and led her to the matron.

During her admittance interview, Annie gave her name as Mary Smith and provided a false history.

~ ~ ~

Annie took a cold bath standing at a basin, with water and rag already used by four other women. She was given to eat a slice of hard bread and a tin cup of thin gruel the inmates called skilly. She took one of the pills the young man at the Union Infirmary had given her, swallowing the medicine with water, then wondered if she was meant to suck on it instead. Next time, she'd taste the tablet before swallowing.

An old, white-haired woman crowded up next to her in the overfilled dining hall reached for the pill box with one hand while using the other to motion toward her mouth. Her eyes spoke of a desperate, yet unfocussed need. Annie struggled with her briefly before regaining control of the medicine. Seeing that the box had cracked, she carefully put the wooden container back into her pocket to keep it together.

Annie rested for the night in a sailcloth hammock in a room full of snoring women, also cocooned in hammocks. The snoring kept her awake as the noise had the last time she'd stayed in the casual ward. She tried to imagine the goodnight kisses her father had given her when she'd been little with the hope that the memory would soothe and somehow help. Unfortunately, the recollection also brought memories of Dadda's cruelty.

As she lay with eyes closed trying to rest without sleep, she wondered about the pitying look Eliza had given her. The woman was no doubt much like Annie, stronger and more forceful, but coming from similar humble circumstances. If not for the competition for Eddie, they might have become friends. Annie fell asleep wishing that were so.

Beau

Shortly after her brother, Fountain, came into the world, when she was twenty years old, Annie met a sweet fellow named James Threwbridge. Despite his awkward bow-legged gait, large nose, and hollow cheeks, she found him attractive because of his bearing and good humor. Dadda had been encouraging her to find a beau and get married, as he said, "before it's too late." She took an afternoon walk with James along Harrow Road on a day in which the sun struggled to emerge from the clouds. As they walked and talked, a drizzle began to fall.

"We should head back to your father's shop," James said.

"It's just rain," Annie said, wanting to prolong their time together.

The rain increased to a downpour and they did turn back. A carriage hurrying by in the road splashed the couple with muddy water.

James offered his wool fitted jacket for Annie to use to dry her wet skirt. Although she didn't think that would help much, she thought he'd made a gallant gesture.

"No, thank you," she said. "My skirts will dry and can be washed later."

"I want you to look your best," he said. "You're a pretty woman."

She knew that wasn't true, but he was not a handsome man, so she'd thought they were well suited. He delighted her most with his ability to tell stories that gave her a laugh.

They arrived at the cobbler shop dripping wet. Her father wasn't in the shop front. Not wanting him to believe that a customer had arrived, Annie called out, "It's just us, Dadda."

With obvious curiosity, James looked over the various benches and tables strewn with tools, sheets and scraps of leather in various colors, grades, and weights, heavy waxed thread, hardware, and glues. He considered the smelly stacks of tagged shoe and boot pairs awaiting repair.

Annie's father emerged from the storeroom at the back of the shop. Relieved to find Dadda sober, she introduced him to James.

"Where does your name come from?" Dadda asked.

"My family comes from Somerset where there's an ancient bridge, the Tarr Steps," James said, showing good cheer. "The Devil is known to sun bathe in the middle of it and keep people from passing over. My Great, Great—several more Greats—Grandfather, a parson, threw the Devil off the bridge to allow people to pass. That's how we got our name."

"What a hero," Annie said. "Are you that kind of brave man, Mr. Threwbridge?"

"Oh, no," James said with a mischievous smile. "I'd have made a deal with the devil. That's the kind of *coward* I am."

Annie and James laughed. Her father merely smiled.

"May I have a word with you?" Dadda asked James.

They retreated to the storeroom. Annie assumed her father spoke to James to offer words of encouragement regarding the young man's effort to court her.

As they emerged, James had an unease about him. "I remembered I must pick up my mother's chair," he said. "The fellow what's weaving a new bottom for it closes his shop early today. I must be off."

"When shall I see you again?" Annie asked.

James glanced at Dadda. "I don't know just now." he turned away and left the shop.

"What did you say to him?" Annie asked Dadda.

"I told James he was good to take you out for a walk."

"No, you didn't," she said, feeling outraged and betrayed. She struck him in the chest with her open hand. "Whatever you *did* say drove him away."

"He were a coward," Dadda said. "He *said* as much. And he were ugly. I won't have homely grandchildren."

Annie never saw James again. She hated her father for that.

Brick Walls
Wednesday, September 5

Annie must have slept some because the next thing she knew, a dour woman in a gray and black uniform was beating on the metal railing that supported the hammocks, sending up a terrible, startling noise.

"Everybody up," she bellowed. "You have work to do."

After another brief meal of bread and skilly, Annie started her work at six o'clock Wednesday morning. She sat on a bench among many other women to begin hours of labor. She picked oakum until her fingers bled.

Helping haul supplies to the kitchen in the early afternoon, she saw her opportunity to escape; a dray entrance had been opened to receive a delivery. The rules of the casual ward required her to stay two nights or forfeit future relief from the poor law union. Having given a false name, she would not be able to return for relief as long as they remembered her face.

She decided she didn't have much choice, and slipped out the door while she had the chance.

~ ~ ~

Annie arrived at Crossingham's in the mid-afternoon. She took that as a time when Eliza would most likely be gone, making her rounds hawking books.

With one penny in her pocket, Annie couldn't pay for her lodgings. She might reclaim her bowl and spoon, though, lost during the fight.

Timothy Donovan's office faced the front entrance to the lodging house. "Come to pay up your room?" he asked in lieu of a greeting. The big man sat at his desk, leaning forward on his elbows, his square chin in his meaty right hand. The chair and desk seemed too small for him.

"No, Tim, haven't got it yet. I was hoping to get some of the lotion in my room." She held up her hands to show him the bloody cracks from picking oakum. "And I misplaced my bowl and spoon. Have you seen them down in the kitchen?"

"You know how it is, Annie," he said, shaking his head, "anything not locked up goes missing."

She nodded sadly.

"You can go to your room for the lotion, but until you've paid up for the night, you can't stay."

Annie nodded again. "May I borrow a key?"

"You haven't lost your key, have you? If you have, it'll cost you two shillings."

"I haven't lost it, just don't have it at present."

"Customers ask for number 29 because the bed is good," he said as he retrieved a spare key for her room. "Should you miss Thursday, you know it'll go fast."

"Yes, Tim."

Annie went up to her room, took a small amount of yellow cream from a jar of thickened sheep's lanolin she'd left on the bedstead. As she rubbed the lotion into her sore hands, she looked at the unmade bed longingly.

Even if Mr. Donovan somehow allowed her to stay without paying up and she locked herself in the room, she feared that Eliza would break in or lay siege until Annie came out, and the beating would be repeated. The woman had said, "Should I see you here again, I'll give you worse."

Annie rubbed a bit more of the lotion into her hands, returned the spare key to Mr. Donovan, and left the lodging house.

She would find the Green Dragon sweatshop and earn what she needed to stay at Crossingham's. Surely, Mr. Donovan wouldn't knowingly allow a paying customer to be molested. She'd held no such hope that the night watchman, John Evans, would defend her the morning of her fight with Eliza.

~ ~ ~

While addled from lack of good food and too little sleep, Annie spent another hour searching for the Green Dragon Sweatshop in Heneage Street. Pausing to rest, she sat with her back to a brick wall.

Just a short rest, John, she thought, *then back to looking for work.*

She imagined him giving her a wink.

In case she fell asleep, she drew her legs in close to keep the foot traffic from stepping on them. The diminished sunlight coming through the coal smoke haze felt warm and drowsy on her face. She would try for sleep, but hunger pangs and the need to find work nagged at her.

Hoping for a taste of sweetness, she took out the little cracked box, extracted one of the white tablets, and put the medicine in her mouth. Finding the pill bitter, she swallowed quickly.

Her rest had lasted only a few minutes when the sight of a woman carrying a basket full of fresh vegetables and walking toward her along the footway brought Annie to her feet. Seeing the basket's contents, particularly the potatoes, her stomach turned over hungrily. The woman dressed as a servant, and probably served one of the jewish families in the neighborhood.

Annie stepped into her path and stopped. "I'm after a sweater in Heneage Street, a finisher of ready-mades." She said the words slowly, trying to prolong the moment of proximity to the food.

The woman had paused, turning to hide the contents of the basket. "I pass through the street on my way to Spitalfields Market," she said, "nothing more."

The load appeared to be heavy and had probably grown more difficult to manage over the long walk. Annie tried to think of something to offer that might help her obtain some of the food. She dismissed, *Should you need to lighten your load, I'd be happy to take a couple of the potatoes*, in favor of, "I should be happy to carry the basket for you for a time."

The woman gave Annie a knowing smile, stepped around her, and walked on. She glanced back once, possibly to make certain she wasn't followed.

Having eaten only the thin skilly and hard bread of the workhouse about ten hours earlier, Annie watched, disappointed, as the basket with the food retreated into the distance.

Couldn't you have asked for one potato? she asked herself. *Does pride stand in the way, or do you merely feel unworthy?* The question wasn't a new one, just unanswered, and, still, she didn't address the matter.

Looking up and down the street, Annie wondered if the sweatshop had moved. Sweaters who ran their shops in tenements often had trouble with their landlords and were forced to relocate.

She searched adjoining streets with no success. The more she looked, the more Annie doubted her memory of the conversation with Amelia.

Either way, a red or green sign, word or picture of a dragon, she could not find the sweatshop. Her disappointment deepened her aching exhaustion. Ironically, she found herself in Hope Street at the moment she'd decided to give up the hunt.

Even here, I come up against a brick wall, she thought as she leaned uncomfortably against another building.

You discourage too easily, my dear. John seemed to say. *You must keep from falling further. Life goes on, and you'll be up to it or suffer more. Don't forget about the girl.*

What girl? she wondered.

No answer came from the fanciful presence within.

Why do I entertain such nonsense? Annie felt strangely resentful, since John gave advice while no longer having to engage in the daily fight for life. Yet hadn't she conjured his ghost in part for that purpose?

Her thoughts had indeed become odd with the fatigue.

He's right, though. I must work hard if I want to see a different future. I shall get out from under Eddie's thumb, and pay fully for my own lodgings. I just have to get through the next few days before making the change. I'll decide what lace sells best, find efficient ways to make more, and work on those day and night until things get better.

So late in the day, her prospects for earning diminished rapidly. She had a single penny of the four needed for her room, and saw only one course left to earn more, an unattractive one best explored at night. To take advantage of the opportunity, she'd need at least a little rest.

Make your way to Saint Mary's churchyard, John seemed to say, *or some park, where you might lie in daylight undisturbed by the constables. Then you may sleep and regain your strength.*

The law permitted sleeping outdoors in daylight. Doing so among the many paupers who dozed in churchyards and parks was a risk, as some merely pretended slumber. Still, she had little of value to lose but her brass wedding ring. That had grown so loose recently that she'd acquired a keeper ring tight enough that she would have good warning should someone try to rob her.

Yes, Annie thought, *Saint Mary's Churchyard wouldn't be a bad spot to rest by day. John always gives good advice.*

Dignity

When Annie was twenty-two years of age, Dadda still slapped and jabbed at her, stomped her toes, pulled her hair, and twisted her ears when he was drunk. She'd learned early on in life that if she complained, his features took on a gleeful look and he redoubled his efforts to abuse her, as if more of the same proved that he meant what he'd done and she should take mistreatment in stride.

At her age, she expected that she should be allowed a certain amount of dignity, so one day while Mum was out and not there to help defend her, Annie fought back.

She'd bent over to adjust the cast iron cheeks in the coal grate with a poker when Dadda reached to smack her on the backside, usually a stinging strike. Out of the corner of her eye, she saw the blow coming, dropped the poker in the embers, and dodged out of the way. "I've had enough from you," she said.

"I'll tell you when you've had enough," he said, leaving his pail of bitter on the table and rising from his chair.

Short of leaving the room, Annie couldn't get away from him. He blocked the way out. She retreated.

"You've always been my favorite," he said, showing his broken teeth and narrowing his eyes, "and you *know* it. So, from time to time, I must put you in your place." His slurred speech told her how drunk he'd become.

He lunged for her, she dodged again, and he went sprawling to the rough floorboards in an undignified manner that seemed to hurt his pride. He pulled a splinter from his left palm as he got to his feet.

The look in his eyes told her she'd suffer worse if she didn't give in and let him hurt her, yet for the first time *her* pride stood in the way. He made a feint that almost fooled her. She tried the same on him with no results. Finally, she dashed into the slot between the bed she shared with her siblings and the one her parents used against the western wall. He followed, and she rolled over her mattress to land on the other side on her feet.

Dadda moved out from between the beds, and lifted the poker from the embers in the coal grate. Annie could see the warp in the air around the hot end of the tool. He swung the iron slowly toward her.

She had to get to the stairs. If she did, she might hop across the missing treads and get out. The stairs always slowed him down, especially when he'd been drinking.

Dadda retreated some and she made a dash for the stairs. He brought the poker around in time to block her passage. The metal bar crossed her chest and the hooked end connected with her left arm above the elbow. The cloth of her chemise burned. Annie heard a sizzle, and smelled her skin burning. She cried out with the pain.

Dadda, looking horrified, dropped the poker and tried to catch her in his arms. Again, she backed away.

"I'm sorry, darling," he said. "I took it too far."

She held her left arm and wept. *He did not mean to do that*, she told herself. *It were the drink.*

With that thought, something, perhaps her heart, turned over inside her and changed her thinking.

No, I shan't give him excuses. Drink or not, he did it. Should I forgive him, he might do worse.

Dadda approached slowly. "I test your love," he said. "I treat you roughly, then look to find again the fondness in your eyes. I don't know why."

Annie backed into the corner by the window, dropped to her knees and defensively covered her head with her arms. Without a word, she looked up at him from between her forearms.

He looked at her in silence for a long moment. His lip trembled, he wiped wetness from his eyes, and fled the room.

From that moment on, Annie considered Dadda dangerous.

Resting Place

By the time Annie got to Saint Mary's Church in Whitechapel Road, about two hours remained before sunset. Once the sun went down, the constables would begin their rounds of rousing paupers from their sleep in parks, churchyards, and cemeteries. She entered the gates with several others who no doubt shared her goal of finding rest. At least two hundred men, women, and children lay upon the ground in the yard. The changing breeze sent the odor of the sleeping horde to sicken Annie. Snoring rose from every quarter.

So many homeless wretches. Who shall I sleep next to? Who among them are here because they wouldn't demean themselves as I've done? How many here have done much worse?

Sleeping near children would perhaps be pleasant, but she knew better than to be insensible beside any not clearly with a parent. Forsaken, homeless children were at least as dangerous as adults, often faster and quieter too.

Annie didn't like to think of children that way. She wanted to love them all, yet her history with her own children had created little more than bad memories.

I am to blame for that, not them.

She saw a young woman with a child cuddled up against her abdomen, a green and blue woolen shawl pulled over them. They slept near the spiked fence in the southwest corner of the yard. Annie saw a space nearby, between a middle-aged soldier and an elderly woman. The white-haired woman clutched a heavy cloth sack of possessions to her thin chest and abdomen as if they were all that kept her afloat in the world. The soldier's right hand was missing. Although his stained and faded blue woolen uniform jacket and trousers had been repaired many times over, they looked ragged. Still, he had no doubt defended the Kingdom somewhere in the world, and with his great barrel of a chest, he appeared to have once had an impressive physique. She would feel safe lying down beside him.

Annie approached the spot, bent and picked up shards of broken glass and tossed them aside, careful not to hit anyone. She brushed away other detritus from the stunted, suffocated grass, and settled to the ground.

The stirred up dust set her to coughing. The soldier opened his eyes and glared at her. Annie held her breath and suppressed the desire to cough. She quietly got out her medicine box, careful not to break the container further, and took one of the pills.

As she lay down, her gaze fell upon the ragged brown shoes belonging to the child cuddled up against the young woman a few feet away. From the pink and gray toes Annie saw peeking out from where a piece of the sole was missing on the right shoe, she thought she recognized the child as female, although she had no real reason to think that.

She thought about her first child, Emily, who she'd called Lily. Annie pictured the girl's first smile, and the soft, callous-free flesh of her newborn fingers and toes. *Sweet girl, I treated you so poorly.*

She used her right arm as a pillow, tucked her left hand under her neck to hide her wedding rings, and closed her tired eyes.

~ ~ ~

The cat's meat man came for her while she slept in the room above the cobbler shop. His sharp, finger-snipping shears, like those she'd seen in the German children's book, *Der Struwwelpeter*, reflected moonlight coming through the window. The bright flash had awakened her.

Annie cried out as he grabbed her, but the sleep of her parents and sister, beside her in the bed, remained untroubled. He took Annie's shoulders in a powerful grip, his grim face, shiny with oil, looming over her in the darkened room. His breath smelled of the rotten, blue meat he sold.

"You must be quiet, so we can sleep," he said with a rather pitiful look in his eye.

The expression confused Annie. Suddenly, he wasn't so frightening. He shook her lightly with one hand. The room from her childhood was gone. She recognized him as the soldier, and knew she lay on the ground in the churchyard.

Annie saw the old woman with the sack glance at her with sympathy, roll over, and draw the sack in tighter.

"I'm sorry," Annie said. "Bad dream."

The soldier let go, and rolled away to go back to sleep.

The young woman and her child—indeed a girl—watched her for a moment, then lay back down.

The sun was retreating behind the buildings to the west.

Annie tried to return to sleep, but had become unsettled.

She got up and left the churchyard, crossed Whitechapel Road, and sat with her back up against yet another brick wall.

What a strange prison I've come to live in.

She'd picked a bad spot to sit down. The traffic in and out of pubs to her left and right made little effort to avoid running into her. Still, she resisted the urge to get up.

Again, she wanted to blame Eliza for her predicament. Even so, she found herself imagining what would have happened had the shoe been on the other foot. If Annie had been capable of overpowering and frightening Eliza away, she'd have done so without considering the consequences for the woman. Indeed, Annie realized that in exposing the theft of the florin, she had intended to destroy the part of the woman's livelihood that involved Eddie. At least Eliza had shown a touch of pity upon seeing Annie in a wretched state, coughing and writhing on the pavement. Annie didn't feel good about her own motives in the matter.

Watching the paupers rouse themselves to leave Saint Mary's Churchyard, Annie dreaded the coming night and the possibility of having to sleep rough. If her mother's lodgings in Brompton were closer, she would go to her and beg for a few hours rest in her room, despite the hard feelings between them. Thoughts of the lodgings at 29 Montpelier Place brought back fond memories. The one room abode, oddly another "29," had been Annie's home for several years, including the time during which she'd courted John. To sleep there again would be a welcomed experience.

Enough—I must bend to the task at hand.

With what precious little time remained to secure her doss for the night, she would find a man willing to pay to lift her skirts. Not opposed to the act on principal, she did find taking a stranger inside her distasteful and took to soliciting as a last resort. When she did, Annie tried to imagine she was with John, but never succeeded.

The first time she'd solicited, shortly after John died and she found herself with no funds, she'd been drunk, which afforded some distance from the act. Even so, she'd experienced such disgust that she'd nearly ruined the moment of release for the client.

"I pay with reluctance," he said. She'd been fortunate he wasn't a pugnacious man.

Each time since had been easier, yet she'd solicited only while drunk, not stone cold sober as she currently found herself. Of course, her intimacy with Eddie had always been a transaction. Before him, Annie had lived with Joseph Sirvey, a maker of wire sieves. Plainly, he'd never had feelings for her. When her husband's funds dried up, Mr. Sirvey had left her.

Too proud to beg, Annie thought with disgust as she stood up, *but not too proud to peddle tail. Well, you'd better get on with it, if you must.*

"Better that than spend a night rough," John said. "Perhaps you'll find the girl."

Startled by a sense of his presence, Annie turned suddenly to look all around her. She saw neither John, nor his ghost.

The voice in her head made no sense. How could she find a girl while soliciting? *Perish the thought!*

Shamed

Mum, carrying Fountain, returned from errands to find Annie smoothing a bit of lard onto her burn.

"What's happened here," Mum asked. She placed Fountain in the bed.

Annie heard her sisters Georgina and Miriam on the stairs, and decided to be brief. "Dadda," she said.

Apparently, that was all the explanation needed. Mum embraced and held her silently for a moment.

The young girls entered the room.

"He's gone out," Annie said, pulling away gently, "and I shouldn't think he'll eat tonight."

Mum helped Annie wrap a strip of blue calico as a bandage around the burned arm.

Emily came in from her work at an industrial kitchen and prepared a supper of stirabout. She showed no interest in Annie's injury. They all ate the hot, milky oatmeal, and Annie told them what happened.

Emily had no comment. She went back out.

As upset as Dadda had been when he left, Annie hoped he'd learned a lesson, yet he arrived home more drunken than she'd ever seen him. He insisted on inspecting the burn on her arm.

Mum swatted him away. "That's enough," she said. "You shall not hurt my daughter anymore." She held Annie in a protective embrace that hurt the injured arm. Annie didn't complain or try to break free.

"Don't coddle your whelp." Dadda said. "Life is hard. I'm trying to toughen her up."

Annie had a few words for him, but knew better that to say them aloud.

"You haven't toughened her, you've harmed her."

"Oh, she put on a great show, she did," he said, "Should I not be allowed to take a look, well then…"

Mum released Annie, leaned toward him and thrust her face up toward his until they stood nearly eyeball to eyeball. "You don't believe her, or you don't remember?"

The vigor of her response surprised him, and he drew back. The second part of her question clearly troubled him. Dadda put away his tongue. He sat at the table and grumbled, his eyes occasionally cutting angrily at Annie as he drank from a pail of bitter.

She contained her anger and did her best to ignore him.

Soliciting

"I'll give you tuppence," the man said.

He and Annie stood at the entrance to a long L-shaped alley off Brick Lane where she hoped to take him for the transaction. Toward the rear of the thin passage, the first-floor windows of the buildings were bricked up. When exploring the place, she'd seen nobody. She had found a short, box-shaped structure with a sloped tin roof over a cellar entrance that would support her comfortably as she bent over for a client.

"That's half the going rate," Annie complained.

"Have you seen your reflection?" he asked.

He was the only one who had shown interest, while the night wore on. With his two pence, she still wouldn't have what she needed to return to Crossingham's or stay in a doss house.

And she found him ugly. He had a huge red nose and rheumy eyes in his over-sized balding head. His blackened, pudgy hands moved restlessly, and she feared what he might do with them.

As Annie considered the price, she remembered how tender she'd been as a child. What would that girl have thought about her current activity?

Poor child. A good thing she did not know.

Thinking about herself with such distance felt odd.

Annie knew she looked bad, but her pride would not allow her to take half the going rate. The moment she said, "No," she knew she'd suffer for the decision.

The man gave her a look of disgust, shook his head, and walked away.

Coldness

The burn scar on Annie's arm disappeared with time; not so the one in her heart. Lacking trust in her father thereafter, considering Dadda a danger, she turned cold to him. When sober, he tried to thaw her heart. Annie rebuffed his efforts. Seeing the hurt look in his eyes, she had sympathy for him, yet knew better than to show it. He ceased to abuse her. Even so, she had little to do with him and rarely said more than a word or two if he spoke to her.

"You must talk with me from time to time," Dadda told Annie. "As your father, you owe me that kindness."

Annie ignored him.

One evening, he brought home an extravagant meal of fried fish, hot green peas and potatoes, and plum duff that he'd bought from street vendors. Annie suspected he intended the food to help him win his way back into her heart.

Dadda watched her as she ate. She kept her eyes on her food as much as possible and tried not to look at him. Plainly, Emily could see what was going on. She excused herself from the table, sat on the bed, and read a book.

Following a long silence, Dadda turned to Mum. "You must persuade your daughter to speak with me," he moaned drunkenly, "to spend time with me."

Emily shook her head and sighed dramatically without looking up from her book.

At eight, six, and four years of age respectively, Georgina, Mirium, and Fountain could ignore the adults with impunity. They dug into the feast with obvious delight.

Dadda hadn't eaten much. He turned away from Annie, and looked out the soot-streaked window. "I've grown so lonely without her," he seemed to say to no one in particular. His eyes brimmed with tears.

Annie could not help looking upon her father with scorn.

~ ~ ~

On Annie's twenty-third birthday in September 1864, she returned home from fetching water at the public pump to find a fine, sky-blue linen skirt, dress bodice, and bonnet laid out on the small bed she shared with Emily. Her drunken father sat at the table with his pail of bitter, a foolish smile on his face.

"For you, darlin'…," he said. Then, he seemed to think for a moment and a smile full of cruel mischief crept over his features. "…so next time, you'll be pretty enough to keep your beau."

Outraged, Annie threw the water from the bucket at her father. She hopped down the stairs and fled down Harrow Road. She wandered the streets for some time, unknown and lost among the countless people she past. The overcast sky, threatening rain with a rumbling of thunder, suited her mood. Although aware of the many voices around her, she truly only heard the one in her head offering bitter things she might say to her father.

You are a cruel man, always have been. You tricked me into loving you so your hatefulness would be more painful. What sort of misery within a man leads him to do such terrible things? Well, I love you no longer.

The last thought hung in her mind uneasily. She did not want to hurt Dadda with those words.

Annie remembered the last glimpse she'd had of him, the hurt in his eyes as he sat in his chair, dripping water.

His manner was hateful. He seemed to have a need to hurt her, perhaps as he'd said, to test her love for him. Might that be because she had not shown him well enough how much she did love him?

The answer hid behind an obstruction of pride. When finally she'd got past it and decided that, indeed, she had not expressed her love properly, she resolved to remedy the situation as best she could. *I shall return home, apologize, and thank him for the gift.*

When she arrived home, Annie found Emily huddled with the smaller children out front of the cobbler shop. A constable stood talking with Mum at the door to the shop, and writing notes in a small book.

"Dadda has done something awful," Emily said as Annie approached. "It's likely your fault."

The younger children were all crying.

Annie could imagine that, in a drunken rage, he might have destroyed furniture in their room or in the shop, or possibly even struck someone. She'd seen him become belligerent to his own customers at times.

"What did he do?" she asked.

Emily struck her in the face, and broke down in tears.

The constable walked away.

Annie approached her mother.

"Your father took his own life," Mum said, a tear in her eye threatening to fall.

The ground at Annie's feet became mush. The doorway to the shop shifted and she clutched at her mother. Mum supported her, kept her from slumping to the stone footway. Annie pulled back to look her mother in the eyes and make certain she had spoken the truth. Mum's gaze held steady. The tear had not fallen.

"It's up to us," she said, "you, me, and Emily, to raise these children. Can I count on you? Your father would want that. Even though he were cruel at times, he worked hard for us, and he did love you."

Annie held her mother and wept.

I am to blame!

Mum gave her time, then said, "You must help me clean up. The others should see no more than they have to."

Reluctantly, Annie climbed the stairs with her mother. Inside their room, she found her father's chair upset in a great pool of blood. The water bucket she'd dropped had rolled toward the southeast corner of the room. Blood had thinned in spots and spread further as it mixed with the water Annie had thrown. Dadda's red hand print appeared at the end of a smear on the rough floorboards.

She wanted nothing to do with the grotesque mess. Still, she knew it was hers to clean up. Mum showed no curiosity concerning the spilled water or the upset bucket, perhaps believing Dadda had spilled it himself.

Thinking that dousing her father had somehow been the insult that brought him to despair, Annie told herself, *I must never tell anyone what I did.*

The two women set about sopping up the mess with rags and wringing them into the bucket.

Dadda's question from a few days earlier rang in Annie's head, "Why will you not speak to me?"

The answer seemed shamefully too simple—she hadn't trusted him anymore. If she'd found a way to forgive him, perhaps he would still be alive.

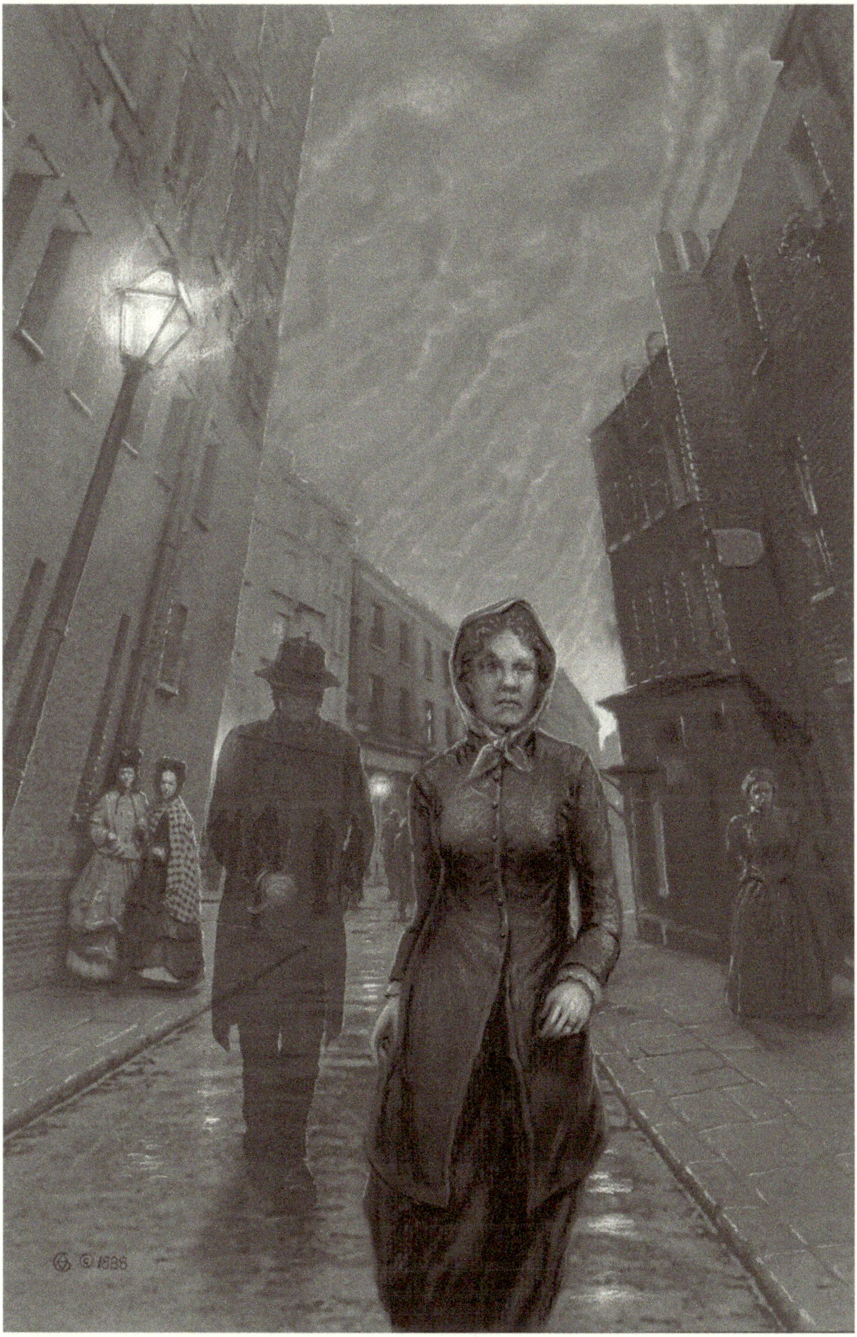

Sleeping Rough
Thursday, September 6

Hearing the bells for two o'clock in the morning, Annie gave up her hunt for a client. All night, she'd faced the possibility of having to sleep rough and she'd slowly become reconciled to the idea. The air seemed unusually cool for early September. Her knee-length black jacket, black stuff skirt, two petticoats, two bodices, neckerchief, and stockings kept her warm enough, but the cracks in the soles of her old boots let the chill in. Annie thought about how, when young, she'd rarely experienced bad footwear because her father kept the family's shoes in good shape.

She had one other way to fortify herself against the night—she retrieved from her pocket the box of medicine given to her at the Union Infirmary, and took one of the tablets. Fumbling in the dark, she feared she dropped a couple of the pills.

Sleeping rough can't be that bad, Annie decided. Then she thought again of the murder of the Nichols woman, and considered returning to Crossingham's and begging her way into the kitchen for an hour's rest. That led her to think of the wild look in Eliza's eyes during their fight. Annie feared the woman more than some unknown murderer.

While Annie had not stayed the night on the streets, she knew the rules well enough from talking with Pearl Watkin's sister, Agatha. If Annie found some hidden spot to doze off and it held an object or a mark in chalk or charcoal, the place was considered taken.

In her hunt for a place to sleep, she found a space between stacks of pallets in a back lane off Whitechapel Road. No public house or tavern backed onto the alley, so there were few rats. Yet the slot between the pallets held a candle stub. Annie imagined settling in to sleep, only to have an angry man, claiming that she trespassed on his lie-down, awaken her. She'd had enough of fighting lately.

If an easy-to-find spot like that had no sign that it had been claimed, most likely the constables knew that homeless tried to sleep there. Her understanding of the law was that she could sit or stand at night in any public place where she wasn't a nuisance, as long as her eyes weren't closed.

Walking along a nearly deserted stretch of Brick Lane, she saw two figures ahead, mere silhouettes in the gloom, one rather tall in a long coat. She heard one of them cry out in a female voice what might have been the word, "murder," cut off. The shorter of the two figures fell. The tall one broke into two parts that then dragged the fallen one—presumably the owner of the female voice—into the darkness of a back lane.

Annie couldn't make sense of what she'd seen, her astonishment leaving her frozen in mid-step until an urgent realization of the need to flee gripped her. She turned and moved quickly in the opposite direction.

The tall one might have been two youngsters pretending to be an adult. Annie had heard that two children working together could be more powerful and dangerous than one man. Guttersnipes were said to have many clever ways to get adults alone and rob them.

I plainly possess nothing of worth, so I'm safe, Annie thought, but she walked for some distance before she became willing to settle in for some rest.

She sat in a recessed doorway, trying to sleep with her eyes open. She couldn't tell if she had any success because the next thing she knew, she was being awakened and asked to move on. She tried the same thing in several other spots; standing up against a building, standing wedged between an open gate and the wooden fence from which it depended, sitting on the front steps of a tenement. She knew she fell asleep, and presumed that eventually, if not immediately, her eyes closed, because she was caught each time. Did any of that constitute rejuvenating repose? If she persisted, would the accumulation of short intervals of sleep become a source of true rest for her? She didn't believe so.

As she continued her search for a place to sleep, she thought of Eliza with a full belly, safe and warm in the room, number 36, at Crossingham's, for which Eddie paid. She would be laughing and having a good time with the man. They would drink and eat, tell bawdy jokes, and eventually make their way to the bed.

Of course, the fun ended there and the bullying began. The good times didn't last long with Eddie. Annie found herself with some sympathy for Eliza as she thought of her own experiences with the man.

Annie cursed her own opportunism. She felt foolish for the way her attempt to turn Eddie against Eliza had backfired. Still, Annie remained indignant at the thought that she suffered for exposing a crime.

The constables who found Annie sleeping often didn't say a word, merely prodded her awake with their truncheons, or shone a bull's eye lamp in her face, and motioned for her to move on.

One who awoke her twice said, "I see you with your eyes closed again, I'll clout you on the head."

A young constable seemed to hold sympathy for her in his eyes. "Move along, please," he said.

Finally, she joined the countless homeless persons shambling miserably along the streets in a stupor, going nowhere, merely kept moving by an ordinance against sleeping rough during the hours of darkness.

Although the connecting avenues running roughly north and south varied quite a bit, Annie most consistently traveled east to west on Whitechapel Road and west to east on Hanbury Street. If seen from overhead, her route, and that of most of the homeless, ran in a clockwise direction.

Oddly, she saw fewer people walking in the opposite direction. When she did encounter someone going the other way, she found the occurrence unpleasant. The possibility of meeting another's gaze disturbed what little rest she got from the dull grind of her walk. Possibly all the tottering homeless found that similarly disagreeable, because, over time, those moving in a counter-clockwise direction became fewer until everyone seemed to be traveling the same way.

The group with whom she'd fallen in—those who happened to travel in the same rough orbit—consisted of an old man ten or more years her senior, a woman with four children of various ages, and a younger fellow who followed at a distance.

Aside from what seemed brief glances to assure themselves that she was harmless, they silently accepted her as a fellow aimless trudging companion. Annie's feet—having gained a mind of their own since the one in her head had become useless—had decided to trust the group not to lead her into danger. She did not have the energy to speak with her chance companions, nor did she bother to make a determination concerning the children, whose ragged clothing gave no clue as to age or gender.

Listening to the footsteps of the younger man following behind, she wondered if she should fear him, but the sound of his tread didn't get any closer. Her few glances back offered little in the dimness.

All seven looked like shadowy ghosts moving through the slight mist and the scant gaslight that illuminated their route at intervals that varied, depending upon which road they walked. The old man held the lead, possibly because the others trusted him to have more experience about which way to go, or merely because he had the longest legs. For a time she found comfort thinking of them as her family, and the young man following as John. She thought of each completed circuit in her orbit as one year of the life she'd had. Listlessly, she wondered if after twenty-seven circuits the young man would catch up, since she'd met John in her twenty-seventh year.

Somewhere along Hanbury Street, Annie saw a small notice, nearly lost among other signage in a first floor window, advertising "cat's meat." Despite the smallness of the sign, she saw it every time she passed by. With each sighting, Annie's old fear of the cat's meat man resurfaced. She'd glance back, and then forget about him, too weary to hold onto her fright.

Periodically, Annie stumbled or stubbed a toe, felt a brief moment of wakefulness, and thought to lie down on the spot and rest until forced to get up. No, she'd only be rudely awakened again. The moments passed quickly and she'd resume her shuffling gait.

Her feet hurt. Her hips and back ached deep in the joints. Her eyes felt swollen in her skull. Each step sent a dull throb through her body to ache dully in her head. Her stomach, a hungry, hollow thing, sank between her hips and sloshed back and forth uncomfortably. A hard kernel of something dreadful and weighty grew in her chest.

Annie desperately needed a way out of the odd, slow torture, but didn't have the presence of mind to find one. If only time would pass more swiftly. She knew from experience that time remained obstinate.

Annie stepped off the kerb at a crossing, took a few steps more, and fell.

Then, Mum was encouraging her to get up. Annie lay in the road. A couple of piles of fresh horse manure had cushioned her fall. The filth saturated her top skirt at the right hip. She saw a wagon and four bearing down on her, the driver giving no indication that he might turn out of her path. As Annie began to rise from the road, her mother's worried features took on a smile.

Light from nearby gas lamp revealed that the woman wasn't Mum.

Sores, probably from lice, became visible at the woman's hair line as she bent closer. Her eyes, sore and bloodshot where they should have been white, oozed milky tears and her purple nose ran. By the look of her—not middle-aged, yet with features creased from hardship—she'd fared much worse in life than had Annie.

What's she got to smile about?

Annie got to the footway with the woman's help and that of her children. She realized that none of them were her family. They moved away without waiting for her thanks, seemingly eager to keep up with the old man, who had continued on and could be seen at least two chains away on the footway.

Never had Annie been more miserable in her life. The kernel had grown, and she felt the lack of sleep as a great stone weight in her chest.

Give me searing pain before this dull, aching misery!

She settled again into a doorway, prepared to resist if told to get up.

A middle-aged policeman awakened her, leaned over and said, "I'll be back this way along my beat in fifteen minutes. You should make the best of that time."

Gratefully, she closed her eyes. When next she saw him, he pointed toward darkness a few feet away from her and said, "Should you take to the shadows beside that building, you'll have another fifteen minutes."

If she did move, Annie couldn't remember.

John seemed to hold her in his arms for a time.

She found herself sprawled in the entrance to a back lane. A driver trying to use the alley to make a delivery had climbed down from his wagon to rouse her. He did so gently. She saw that the sky beyond his silhouette had grown brighter, that night had ended.

Again, she experienced gratitude. She got up and wandered along the footway, trying to determine her position within the East End.

As the sun rose high enough to reach and illuminate her body, she slouched down against the nearest building to rest. She saw several others on the street do the same before she closed her eyes.

~ ~ ~

When Annie next became aware of her surroundings, she was surprised to see the sun halfway down the western sky. She'd been allowed to rest on the street for most of the day.

Getting up and moving along the road, she wondered if the morning had brought a more merciful world, one full of kindhearted people. She thought of the woman and her children who had helped her out of the road, the constable who'd given her fifteen minute intervals of sleep, and the driver who had gently awakened her

Could it be that life will become easier?

As she entered a street crossing, the driver of an approaching van shouted, "Out of the way, cumberground!"

She gasped and stepped back to avoid being hit, as the vehicle hurried by.

Annie supposed that she had her answer.

Glue

George Smith had cut his throat with one of his cobbler knives.

As punishment for what she saw as her role in his death, Annie gave herself a sentence of five years tedious labor.

The cobbler shop came under new management and the Smith family removed to humbler lodgings; a single, windowless room in a drafty old wooden house that held six other families at 29 Montpelier Place, Brompton. Within the ten by fifteen foot chamber, they fit the two beds, armoire, hutch, table and three chairs hauled from the room above the cobbler shop in Harrow Road.

Mum had wanted to leave behind the newer, smaller bed, the one Annie shared with her siblings. "Better to crowd the room than crowd the bed," she said after deciding otherwise. "With growing children, we'll need it."

Montpelier Place existing in an area of mixed classes, the family encountered more people who looked upon them with disdain. The walk to the public pump for water took longer than what they'd been used to in Harrow Road. The chimney flue in the room didn't draw well at times, and they all suffered chronic coughs.

Annie felt responsible for the hardship her family suffered. She did her best to compensate, helping her mother find work and contributing to the household any way she could. Emily treated her coldly for a few months, then her anger eased up.

Mum, Annie, and Emily took jobs as scourers during the day at Price Laundry. They also took in piece work to be done in the evenings. They applied hundreds of thousands of labels to boxes, jars, and bottles, and made many thousands each of paper bags, paper boxes, and wooden matchboxes.

"Surely the world will run out of glue before we're done," Mom complained one night. "Then we'll be out of work. I could think of worse things."

They had boxes of tiny bottles stacked against two walls, four rows deep, and rows of the vessels laid out on the two beds to dry. Georgina unpacked the boxes and handed Emily bottles one at a time. The three adult women sat working at the table. Emily dipped a small brush into a pot of amber-colored glue, spread the slightly thick liquid onto a label, and handed that to her mother. Mum carefully affixed each one to a bottle, and handed that to her eldest. Annie wiped away any excess glue with a damp rag, careful not to touch and make the ink run, then handed the bottle to Georgina who found a place to set the vessel on one of the beds or on the floor to dry. Georgina also repacked the boxes with bottles once their labels had dried.

For every two hundred bottles, they earned one penny. While, at that rate, the labor remained worthwhile, they frequently ran out of room and had to suspend their work until the vessels spread throughout the abode had dried enough to be repacked or until a finished load had been picked up by the manufacturer and a fresh one delivered.

The labels proclaimed, "Dr. Fulsome's Liver Cleaner, the only medicine ever needed! Cures rheumatism, pleurisy, digestive disorders, and gout. Wards off consumption, cholera, small pox, measles, mumps, and rubella, as well as hundreds of other dread diseases. Dose for children, one teaspoon. Dose for adults, two teaspoons. To be taken daily."

The little bottles looked as if they might hold about eight teaspoons of liquid.

"We shan't run out of glue," Emily said. "Horses only live about three years on London streets. So Harry tells me." Her beau, Harry Chambers, was a carman for a railway station. He lived in a mews at the station and always smelled pleasantly of horses. "By the hundreds, their carcasses are hauled off the streets to the glue factory every day."

"Why do they die so young?" Mum asked.

"Many meet with accidents, but more are simply worn down by the stone roads. It's so hard on their joints, says Harry."

"Poor creatures," Annie said.

"Yes," Emily said. "That's what he thinks. He's good to his horses, and tries to give them a good life, short as it is."

Annie wondered how many horses she'd gone through applying labels and making boxes and bags.

If the source for the glue didn't run out, periodically the need for the products did. They took in mending, and did knitting piece work as well, producing endless socks, mittens, and sweaters.

When the skin of Mum's hands began to crack open with bleeding sores in 1866, she left Price Laundry and took up childminding. From Monday to Friday, the bawling babies and mischievous toddlers of at least five clients at a time took over the Smith family room from seven o'clock in the morning until seven o'clock at night.

The family could no longer take in piece work that involved glueing. The space that would have been taken up storing boxes, they needed for the children. The Smiths stuck with knitting.

Again, time demonstrated its obstinate nature, passing too slowly during the tedium of labor, and too swiftly as Annie saw herself headed toward spinsterhood. The days of work, the weeks of toil, the months of drudgery, all done for her family, became a yoke that Annie had to cast off.

When Georgina reached eleven years of age in 1867, she left school and began to contribute to the household income, also working at Price Laundry. Annie decided she could take a bit of time for herself at that point and on occasion went to a pub in the evening to be with friends with whom she worked at the laundry.

"Careful with the drink," Mum warned her. "You saw what it did to your father."

"I stay away from strong drink, Mum. I have a glass of bitter, ale, or stout, nothing more. We talk, sing songs, gossip, tell stories, and flirt. It's all quite harmless."

Although she could not have looked forward to losing a bread-winner to a possible future husband, Mum had smiled to hear the word "flirt."

Once Annie's outings to pubs had become a regular habit, her mother showed further concern. "You go *every* night, now."

"If I must labor all day, every day," Annie said, "I deserve to spend some of the night with a glass of bitter."

She looked forward to the evening of each day, when she could leave her drudgery behind. The mild drink helped her relax and occasionally provided a welcomed euphoria. Annie would not allow her mother to take that away from her.

Begging

Annie spent what remained of Thursday's daylight begging. She might still have been unworthy. No longer was she too proud.

She took up a station near Christ Church and appealed to those coming and going from Spitalfields Market. She had no tale of woe that could be told quickly, nor did she possess a gift for language, so she took the practice she'd seen many times among beggars of communicating with facial features alone. Her physical condition, especially with the bruises, and her worn clothing were an asset. A pathetic, imploring look got her some small notice, especially from the middle-aged women walking by on the street. She made subtle changes in her expression until she thought she got the best results under the circumstances.

If a woman walked with a man, most often he dragged her away from Annie. One flaxen-haired woman in a pink linen skirt and white bodice argued for a moment with the man accompanying her, possibly her husband, who tried to do that. Annie didn't hear what she said, but she did hear the man. "How do you know if she is one of the deserving poor?" he said. In his gray bowler, gray and brown checked wool jacket, waistcoat, and trousers, he was dressed quite well for the neighborhood. He didn't bother to hide his contempt. The woman gave one last look at Annie, and turned away with the man.

Annie wanted to spit on the pavement in the direction they'd taken, and then thought better of expressing her anger.

An elderly woman coming from the church took an interest in Annie. Of a middling station, and clearly quite comfortable, she had eyes creased from years of warm expressions. "My dear," she said with sympathy in her eyes, "how did you happen to be so injured?"

Annie knew the woman referred to her bruises. "My husband took up with another woman, beat me, and turned me out in the street." Annie felt odd involving John in a lie. He would never have treated her that way. *Forgive me, John.*

"Do what you must, dearest," he said. "Nothing in that world can harm me any longer."

Annie grew excited as the woman pulled out a purse.

"May this help a little," she said, and handed over a farthing.

Yes, a very *little*, Annie thought, yet she said, "Thank you," then added as an afterthought, "God bless you, Madam."

The woman smiled, pulled her pretty crocheted shawl higher on her shoulders, and walked away.

Annie realized she'd made that shawl. She hoped the beautiful thing kept the woman warm.

In the two hours before dark, Annie received funds from two more people, a ha'penny from a young woman wheeling a babe in a perambulator, and another farthing from a man in some sort of railway company uniform. If she had another six hours, perhaps she could earn what she needed to pay up her room, but with the fading of the light, the crowd thinned, and Annie became discouraged.

~ ~ ~

Upset by the thought that she'd loose number 29 if she didn't pay up that night, Annie knew she must find a client at a rate of two pence if need be. Feeling wholly unattractive, she began a circuit of public houses with the hope of catching a man's eye. Once inside a place, if she didn't buy a drink or find someone quickly who was willing to ask her to sit with him, she'd be turned out in the street. In the Cock and Hoop in Gun Street, she saw a tall, balding fellow sitting alone in a corner nodding in her direction.

The publican approached in that moment. "You must have something or leave," he said.

Annie turned to him, considering how to delay her expulsion. The portly fellow looked strong enough to force her from the premises with little effort.

"I'll have a glass of stout," she said quickly.

He fetched her drink from his man behind the bar, and took a penny from her.

Annie looked again for the tall, bald fellow in the corner.

He was gone.

Annie had spent all of her earnings from begging on that glass of stout. She cursed herself. Now she'd have to earn at least three pence on a client.

At the Cross Keys pub in Wentworth Street she saw a fellow sitting at a table wearing a black hat. Since he wore the hat indoors, she identified him as Jewish. Annie made eyes at him, and he motioned for her to join him. As she move to his table, a few heads in the busy place turned to watch her with disdainful eyes.

"You look like you need a drink and something to eat," he said with a light foreign accent. "You've had it hard lately?" He folded his hands and frowned in sympathy.

"Yes, I have," she said, hoping that he meant to buy her those things. Sitting across from him, Annie gestured toward her face and clothes. "I am not accustomed to being like this, but a woman attacked me, and I lost my lodgings Tuesday. I slept rough last night."

"I am too full of the lush to care about appearances," he said, his speech slurred.

She didn't like the response. She preferred to think he'd chosen her. Yet how could he have done, given her condition? Of course, he looked none too clean himself, with his shabby clothes, black-stained fingers, stove-in hat, and the half growth of beard encroaching on his otherwise well-formed mustache.

No, I shan't be like that. I am fortunate that he asked me to sit with him.

"I am Mr. Wess," he said. "Your name?"

"Annie."

"What shall you have, Annie? They have a nice pea's soup."

"Yes, that sounds good," Annie said, then added apologetically, "and I like rum."

"Ah, so do I."

He motioned for a barmaid who stood in the corner of the room. As the woman fetched the order, he spoke again.

"I've a woman hawks my books," he said, "nearly lost her lodgings last week. Life is precarious for all of us in the East End. There could be riots at any time."

Could he mean Eliza? Annie tried to think of a way to find out without revealing her relationship with the woman. If Eliza had told him about their fight, he might hold hard feelings toward Annie.

"The man who pays for her lodgings returned from being away and placed certain unsavory—no, I should say debauched and unnatural—conditions on her further use of the room at the lodging house. When she balked, he threatened to have her turned out in the street. She'd recently lost her mum and spent what she had to have the woman buried in hallowed ground."

That sounded much like an experience Annie had had with Eddie over placing his manhood in her backside and other indignities he'd demanded. She could not understand his fascination with that part of the anatomy.

"I require you to insert a finger into my bung hole while you suck me," he'd said to her one night.

She'd been drunk enough to comply without becoming too ill, yet the act disgusted her. After that, having her digit in his arse became a requirement every time she sucked his manhood.

Later, he'd wanted something more. "Tonight you shall lick it."

Had anyone ever done such a thing and survived? She imagined she might take in a disease, one like phossy jaw that women who worked at match factories suffered. She'd seen women with the illness, their teeth exposed through gaping holes in their cheeks. The thought horrified her.

Even so, for the sake of keeping her room, Annie had tried to do as Eddie asked, but gagged on the odor, and ended up vomiting into the cleft of his arse.

The anger and disgust on his face had frightened Annie. She'd thought she was done for, that he'd beat her. Instead, he hastily cleaned at the basin and dressed. "I should go to Brummy to have you ejected from Crossingham's this very night," he shouted.

Annie apologized in every way she could think to do so, and eventually his anger cooled. Thankfully, he didn't ask for that particular indignity again.

Yes—Mr. Wess must have been talking about Eliza. Realizing that Eliza no doubt went through the same sort of demeaning acts, Annie's sympathy for her deepened. She knew well the feelings that went with sacrificing personal dignity in order to get on in life.

And she'd just lost her mother. Annie began to understand better the feelings behind the wild look in Eliza's eyes the night of their fight. *Fear and loss drove her terrible attack.*

Apologies to the Cat's Meat Man

Annie ate her soup and sipped her rum. Mr. Wess talked about the political pamphlets he published, his voice becoming increasingly slurred as time went on. Once she'd finished her food and drink, he ordered more rum for each of them. Although Mr. Wess seemed to want a companion, she found no hint in his demeanor that he wanted sex.

He talked about the power laborers had to join together, speak with one voice, and demand changes in employment policies. Annie wondered how he could expect hundreds of thousands of poor people, possibly millions, to ever agree on what to say, let alone speak up, when the competition for jobs was so fierce. Employers had workers over a barrel much the way Eddie did Eliza and Annie. If the man said bend over, they had to comply or find themselves in the street. Desperation compelled them to make choices against their own interests.

Annie wasn't the least interested in Mr. Wess's unreasonable hopes or political views, yet she remained content to keep company with so generous a fellow. She nodded her head and made certain that she appeared to listen, even if her thoughts were at times far away.

Mr. Wess grew so drunk that he finally fell insensible, his head upon the sticky table. Annie sat with him as long as she could to forestall returning out into the night. She tried to think of a way to get his head back upright, and keep his eyes open. None of the methods she thought of seemed reasonable.

Eventually the publican, another large man with a thick middle, roused Mr. Wess. "Out you go, and take your dollymop with you." Annie bristled at the publican's slight, even though her pursuit did indeed invite the term. He gripped Mr. Wess under the arms, lifted him to his feet, and escorted the couple outside.

Annie watched Mr. Wess stumble away southward into George Yard. Briefly, she considered following and robbing him in the darkness of the thin lane—he'd never know the difference. But she knew she couldn't do that to anyone, let alone a man who had been generous to her without asking anything in return.

She wandered the streets again, fearing a repetition of the night before. The fear intensified as a rain began to fall. Just before the bells for three o'clock in the morning, a commotion in an alley behind a warehouse in Commercial Street attracted her attention. Peeking around a corner, she saw two men struggling to roll a tun out of the warehouse through a dray entrance. Annie hid in the shadows until they retreated back inside, then approached the giant barrel. The head boards at one end were loose. She pulled them aside and crawled in.

Lying on the hard oak staves, listening to the rain drumming softly on the outside of the vessel, Annie knew a deep weariness from the rigors of the last few days. While grateful to have found a sheltered lie-down, she considered a question that always brought her a chill: *Is life worth living?*

She knew that in increasing numbers, Londoners, especially women, took their own lives. Life had become harder for Annie each year that she'd been alive, and she suspected the same could be said for just about everyone she knew. The faces around her day in and day out were worn, lined with worry, their eyes turned inward with pain.

A month earlier, Annie had been on her way to Vauxhall to try to beg money from her sister, Emily, when she'd seen a young woman fished dead out of the River Thames beneath London Bridge. She had never seen an expression more peaceful than the one on the face of the corpse.

That's because she faced no future at all.
Perhaps that is desirable.

Annie knew she bore responsibility for her present predicament, and the shame of that wore on her more than fatigue and hunger. To hide her responsibility from herself and others, she'd allowed a plausible lie to stand in for the truth. The lie was that she'd told Eddie about Eliza taking his florin because she hadn't wanted him to suffer the theft, when in truth her intention had been purely to destroy the woman's relationship with the man. Pitifully, she'd been ready with the lie for anyone who might have questioned her motives, yet no one had, except for Eliza in her own dramatic way. Hadn't Annie known that no one would think Eliza worth defending?

The two women were much the same. Annie considered her dissembling in defense of what she had done with Eddie—the demeaning acts she had endured, but she would never find acceptable—the most shameful part of the whole affair.

How can I trust myself? Am I so afraid of the street that I'll do anything? In the future, what shall I find myself doing just to get by?
Shall I wait to see what more I'll have to endure?

Perhaps life wasn't worth living if it continually bent her over such hard choices. One final choice could end the shame, the guilt, the regret, and the daily hardship. Annie had toyed with the idea of suicide several times in recent years. Remembering the terrible emotions surrounding her father's death always drove her away from truly considering the act.

Annie's thoughts and feelings ran in circles as she tried to find sleep. She found hope in imagining freedom from woe, a thoughtless rest, a release from crippling memory. She also found a fear of deep, dark emptiness, the inevitability of being forgotten, a frightful sense that her life meant nothing, and the dreamless sleep she'd dreaded in childhood. She imagined becoming disembodied regret, a ghost wandering forever without rest.

The dreadful thoughts would not go away until she promised herself that she would seriously consider the matter. She would have to think about what life offered and weigh that against…what, nothingness?

Yes.

The promise had an effect on her similar to that of the kisses she had received at bedtime when little. Her mind emptied and she relaxed.

John

When Annie and John were a young couple, brought together in part by their desire for drink, he'd loved the little girl within her. "You giggle like a delighted child at my jests!" he told her. John had known how to draw that child out with good humor, and Annie had loved the feeling it gave her.

They'd met at a pub in Brompton Road on an evening in April of 1868. Annie would always be grateful to Ellen Webster for making that possible.

Annie had become friends with the impressive young woman at Price Laundry. Though twenty-five years old, Ellen held a clerk position at the establishment, one in which she was trusted to take money from customers, keep accounts, and pay employees. Annie discovered that Ellen and her family, likewise missing a patriarch, had taken residence in a much better lodging house across the street from the one the Smith family occupied in Montpelier Place. She belonged to a higher station—her father had done well for himself as a clerk of works in construction until a crane fell on him—and yet she didn't display a superior manner. Annie liked the idea of having a friend so close by. They went to pubs together in the evenings.

One afternoon, Ellen stopped at the Smith lodgings to deliver overdue wages to Annie, Emily, and Georgina.

"I'm sorry for the tardiness," she said, handing over a sum of five shillings, three pence to each of them. "You know Mr. Price requires me to make employees suffer the delays when too many customers are in arrears."

"It's never been a hardship," Mum said.

Annie knew her mother only said that because of Ellen's higher station. The delays didn't mean serious hardship, but the family had gone without meat on occasion because of them. Annie didn't blame Ellen.

"Would you go with me tonight to the Frizzin and Flint," she asked Annie.

Annie was accustomed to rougher public houses than that. The Frizzin and Flint Tavern had a variety of drinking boxes and private rooms that attracted those of a higher station.

"If you're with me," she said, "we'll find ourselves in the lower class section." Annie was embarrassed to have to say so.

"I want to see what the place is like," Ellen said. "Don't you?"

Annie remained uncomfortable with the idea. "I wouldn't have anything to wear."

Ellen turned to Mum who sat replacing a button on a skirt, the fine, sky-blue linen one Dadda had given Annie the day he died.

"That one is fine," Ellen said.

"It belongs to Emily," Annie lied, giving slight warning looks to her sister and mother. She hated the skirt, bodice, and bonnet her father had given her. The hem of the skirt, stained with a spatter of his blood, had been replaced with a strip of cloth that didn't quite match. She couldn't help but think of her father's death when she wore the dress.

"You'll borrow one of mine, then," Ellen said.

Her friend's expression was so earnest, Annie lost her trepidation. She smiled, feeling great warmth toward Ellen.

~ ~ ~

Annie's first introduction to the pub wasn't a good one. Someone sickened had vomited near the entrance. Although sawdust had been thrown down and the mess swept into a corner, the odor nearly drove Annie away. Not wanting her strong reaction to the smell to become an embarrassment, she held her breath and followed her friend inside.

Ellen seemed to sense her distress, and steered her to the back of the pub, as far from the entrance as possible.

Annie took in the atmosphere of the place. The Frizzin and Flint had all sorts of firearms; pistols, muskets, rifles, and a few more exotic types, many of which had neither frizzin nor flint, bolted to the walls.

"The publican told me that all the weapons have been rendered inoperable," Ellen said.

Dingy and full of the odors of food, drink, and tobacco smoke, the pub didn't appear much different from others Annie had visited, except for the decorations and the finer quality of clothing worn by some of its patrons.

They found a table, but Ellen didn't sit. "I shall get you a glass of rum," she said.

"No, the bitter will do."

"I'll just be a moment." Ellen moved to a barmaid delivering drinks to another table, spoke to her and pointed toward Annie. Then she left, possibly to visit the privy.

Annie overheard a fellow at the next table drunkenly extolling the virtues of the rifle hung above his table. He reclined lengthwise on the bench against the wall in the corner of the room, leaning back with his feet up, while his companions sat across the table from him. "I carried her throughout my time in the New Zealand Land War." He reached up and touched the firearm with obvious affection.

Annie thought him either drunk or a fool to be so adoring of the weapon. He had a handsome look, in a boyish way, with light brown wavy hair, close cropped mutton chops, and an otherwise clean-shaven face. The clothing under his jacket appeared to be a livery of some sort. Perhaps he worked in the service of some local family.

His companions, two men and a woman, seemed the worse for drink. One of the men, a fellow wearing the same livery, snored lightly, his head resting on the damp, pitted table, his arms threaded haphazardly between several empty glasses. Annie cringed to see the fluids oozing from his nose and mouth, and withdrew her own arms from the table at which she sat.

The other man, a handsome bearded fellow, busied himself caressing and kissing the woman. She struggled to keep her head of orange hair out of their mouths as they canoodled. They were clearly more interested in each other than in listening to their companion.

The fellow talking about the rifle tore his gaze from the firearm, glanced at Annie with a soft smile, and turned back to his disinterested audience with more of his recollections, seeming content to be the only one listening to his tale.

"I found her as good a companion as a man could want, not a bit fussy. Feed her a greased cartridge, ram it in hard,"—he paused to pantomime the action—"fit a cap onto her nipple," —he made a light pinching motion with his left hand—"and she became ready and willing."

While she remained uncertain as to his mood, Annie covered her mouth to stifle a giggle.

Noticing her reaction, he turned to her with a knowing smile, then grinned.

"She held her warmth after a long day of fighting," he said, idly reaching up to caress the butt of the rifle as he looked Annie in the eye, "and I'd cuddle up to her when I slept at night."

Annie laughed out loud, and he grinned again. She saw that he had most of his front teeth.

He became serious suddenly. "May I sit with you, miss?" he said. "My companions have no need of my jests, yet you have the good humor of a young girl." His gaze fell on her in a way that Annie liked.

"Do you dare part from your lover," she asked.

Glancing at the weapon again, he frowned comically. "She's not the forgiving sort…" He shook his head slowly with a grave expression. "…but she's hard of hearing and currently looking away." He grinned and pointed the same direction as the firearm's barrel; into the corner. "She'll never know I'm gone."

Annie gestured for him to join her.

He lifted his glass, moved to her table, and sat across from her. "My name is John Chapman. I've never been to New Zealand. I did hear a fellow in here the other night going on about the rifle in that manner. Funny, he were."

"My Mother's maiden name is Chapman."

"Perhaps we're cousins."

Ellen returned with two glasses, gave Mr. Chapman a skeptical look. She sat down next to Annie, and passed one of the glasses to her. "She was too slow, so I fetched them myself."

Annie worried that the barmaid had decided she didn't belong in that part of the tavern, then shook the thought off.

"This is my cousin, John," she said, gesturing.

Ellen seemed to relax, and Annie gave John a conspiratorial smile.

Her glass didn't hold much liquid, and she wondered if Ellen had drunk most of her bitter. Raising the drink to her mouth, she got a powerful odor and her eyes went wide.

"Rum," Ellen said. "It's about time you had a grown woman's drink."

John turned to Annie. "Never had rum?"

"Of course I have," Annie said, not wanting to disappoint him. She gave Ellen a quick glance, then turned up her glass and downed the contents.

The burn in Annie's mouth and throat took her by surprise. She turned away coughing, and sat gulping air, waiting for the sensation to subside. Despite the pain of swallowing the stuff, she liked the flavor the drink left in her mouth.

Ellen had a guilty expression even as she grinned at Annie's response to the drink.

"Their rum is very good, indeed," John said, laughing as he offered a linen handkerchief.

Annie waved away the remaining fumes, bringing herself under control, and refused the handkerchief.

"And how is my sweet aunt?" John asked.

Annie fanned her face with a hand as she considered playing along. "She-she's well and happy. And my aunt?"

Annie saw further conspiracy in his eyes. "She's well, but for being pixilated." He shook his head with a somber expression.

Ellen gave him a half-smile, as if she waited for John to laugh at his own joke.

"Oh, yes," Annie said with a look of concern, "I saw her at market not a week ago with bite marks all over her. She said she had bedbugs again, a much worse infestation than before."

"It's the shame that makes her lie," John said. "I trust you two can keep the secret."

Ellen frowned, a frustrated, worried look on her face, as John nodded with a serious expression.

"Do the pixies bite her only at night?" Annie asked.

"You don't truly believe—" Ellen began

John cut her off. "Yes, they come in her sleep."

"They *must* be bedbugs, then," Ellen said with a self-satisfied smile.

Feeling the rum, Annie became more mischievous. "Would that it were bedbugs," she said in all seriousness.

"Yes," John said, "once they've put enough venom in her, she'll commit crimes for them without a thought. As it is, I have to return the belongings she steals from the neighbors, apologize for her, and beg for mercy. So far none have brought charges. I fear it's only a matter of time."

"Ha," Ellen said, "you expect I'm a fool."

"Oh, no," John said. "Most people in London don't believe, but I spent my youth in the fields and stables around Newmarket. All the stables had charms on them to keep the pixies out. They still got into the haylofts. I had to chase them out, and one of them got me." He rolled up his sleeve and exposed a scar that looked like a bite had been taken from his arm. "With that bite when I were sixteen years old, I found myself hoisting chops from the butcher at market. Magistrate give me two months hard labor."

Ellen seemed to consider his tale.

Annie felt warm inside, and the drink had loosened her tongue. "That Fenian, Barrett, what will hang at Newgate next month," she said. "People who know, say it were pixies made him set that bomb. He's got bite marks all over his legs and chest, just under his clothes."

"Oh my," Ellen said, wide-eyed. She knit her brow, and looked into her drink as she seemed to consider the possibility.

Annie laughed, and John joined her.

Ellen looked angry for a moment, then laughed at herself. "You nearly had me fooled with your story.

"We did have you!" Annie said, embracing Ellen.

"My mother told me tales of fairies when I was a girl," Ellen said, smiling shyly. "I always wanted them to be true and tried hard to believe, as she said I should."

John caught the attention of the barmaid and ordered more drinks.

"You two must have practiced what you'd say," Ellen said. "You're so very clever." She shoved her right shoulder into Annie's left one.

"No, no," John said. "We've never met before."

"And now you expect I should believe that."

Annie and John looked at each other. They'd never met before that night, yet somehow she did know him. John had a friendly face, one full of warmth and good cheer. No man had ever looked at her quite like he did in that moment. She saw in his features a desire for her, a look that held an enthusiastic respect as well as a sexual need.

He'd said that she had the good humor of a young girl, but she wasn't used to laughing, and could do with a lot more of it.

"I suspect you two will be seeing a lot more of each other," Ellen said. She smiled, looking under her brow at them, her tone holding a slight edge of worry.

Annie found herself nodding as she looked at John. His eyebrows arched and he also nodded with a big grin.

Later, she would understand that much of her friendliness and good cheer that night had come with the dose of rum. Far from considering that a cause for concern, she wondered how she'd got along in life without strong drink. She began to rethink much of what she'd believed about her father's drinking. Surely, something that made one feel so good had not inspired her father's cruelty and ultimately led him to take his own life.

Annie met John at a pub nearly every night in the year that followed. She learned that he did quite well for himself as a coachman in the service of Mr. Edwin Ward, a self-made man in the underground construction trade. Like Ellen, John seemed to think little of the fact that Annie had next to nothing in life. His delight with the little girl in her brought out the little boy in him. With an innocent abandon, Annie and John drank, shared good humor, and became inseparably close.

They wed on the first day of May, 1869, at All Saints Church, Knightsbridge.

Dream
Friday, September 7

Annie awoke on Friday with a savory flavor from her dream still on her tongue. Her stomach growled and she looked for more of the food, but held nothing in her hands.

A yeasty odor of drink in the darkness brought back memory, and she knew she lay in the empty tun behind the warehouse in Commercial Street. Not wanting to be there, she tried to return to her dream. She must hold onto the beautiful vision. Once the dream was gone, she'd have to face the dark and frightful choice.

What choice?

No, she couldn't think of that now. Indeed, something about the dream would allow her to stave off the decision. She knew she must recollect the dream's details, even as the sounds of people talking and moving around in the alley outside the barrel came to her through the bung hole to her right, increasing her awareness of the waking world.

Ah! A bit recalled—Annie had flown over London, alighting wherever she wanted. She'd found herself returning again and again to the bloodless market, Covent Garden, where she smelled the abundance of fresh flowers, fruits, and vegetables. She received welcoming looks from all who saw her and they seemed to think little of the fact that she could fly. Flower girls gave her lilies, pinks, violets, and wallflowers. A woman selling hot food from a barrow gave Annie a salted, larded potato.

That had been the warm flavor on her tongue when she awoke. Now, the fatty potato flavor was gone and her mouth held merely the bitterness gathered in sleep.

And again, she found of immediate, nagging importance the need to choose between one thing and another. Annie must sort, weigh, and choose…*between what?* While trying to rest last night, too tired to sleep, she'd struggled to find the willingness to make a choice. The "what" had been clear at the time. Finally, with a promise to herself to address the decision, sleep had come. Now, of the utmost importance, her choice must follow!

But, like the dream, the substance of the pending decision fled her sleepy, grasping thoughts.

Damn my forgetfulness!

Food. Once she had something inside her, she'd remember.

She pushed on the head and cant boards she'd fitted in place at one end of the giant barrel. They fell aside and daylight shone in. As she emerged from the vessel, a young couple passed by holding hands, laborers from the looks of them.

"Homeless now sold by the tun," the young man said looking back. His female companion joined him in mocking laughter.

Annie pretended to ignore them.

The position of the brighter spot in the hazy sky overhead suggested afternoon.

A wonder I kept the sleeping spot for so long without challenge. She'd been so tired when she found the tun, she hadn't questioned her good fortune. Come evening again, the barrel would be gone, sent off to be refilled. If somehow the tun did stay, another pauper would find it and claim the spot as a lie-down, as she'd done.

Even so, since she'd lost her room at Crossingham's, she'd look for the tun come nightfall on the odd chance that it remained available. If so, what she might earn that day could be spent on food instead of lodgings at a doss house.

"The girl sent you the dream," John said. "You ought to talk with her before you make that fateful decision."

The choice? Fateful?

Ah, yes—Suicide! That's it. To be or not to be, yet nothing as grand as our great poet would have written.

The dreadful choice hinged on the simple question: Is life worth living?

Again, she asked John, *What girl?*

"You'll know her when you find her," he said.

With questions left unanswered, Annie had the odd sense that she'd lost control of her imagination, that fancy—John's ghost—had taken on a life of its own. Preferable to the idea that she suffered an encroaching madness was accepting that his ghost truly visited.

Nonsense. I need to eat something to right my head!

Disappointments

Annie continued to live with her mother for a time since her marriage to John had to be kept from his employer, Mr. Ward. Because the gentleman lived at Buridge's Hotel, and wanted to be able to travel from there at a moment's notice to any of a number of job sites, he'd had John installed in the hotel's mews and required him to live there. Mr. Ward insisted that all his servants should remain unmarried. John's accommodations above the stables were modest, but comfortable, something to which he'd become accustomed. If Annie wanted a romp in bed with her husband, he got them a room at an inn.

~ ~ ~

"I'm knapped," Annie said, trying to show a brave face.

She and Ellen sat enjoying glasses of stout at the Fulham Bridge Public House on Brompton Road on an evening when John was on duty. Annie liked the place for the green glass in the windows and the polished red wood, possibly cherry, of the bar, and other furnishings.

"Congratulations," Ellen said. "That's wonderful news. What did your mum and John have to say?"

"Mum says there's not enough room."

Annie chuckled sadly, and Ellen smiled.

"John, he couldn't be happier. We strolled through Brompton Square when I told him. He did a back flip, and walked on his hands, hooting and singing out, 'I'll be a father!' Frightened the fine ladies walking the path. A governess and her charge were delighted." Annie gave a fleeting smile.

"*You* don't look very happy about it."

"I'm frightened. I saw what Mum went through with Georgina, Mirium, and Fountain."

"They say that after the child is born, you don't remember the labor well."

"I don't want to talk about it. I'm sorry for bringing it up."

"Don't be *silly*!" Ellen remained quiet for a moment, watching Annie, then said, "looks like your ship is stuck in the doldrums."

"I see John more now than before we married," Annie said, "not much more, but still more, and yet I'm lonelier than before."

"Of course you are," Ellen said. "He's yours, and you can't have him."

"Yes, I suppose that's it."

They talked about those with whom they worked—who among them could or couldn't sing, who got into the most trouble with drink and men, who the other laborers resented most for their laziness, and how much harder everyone had to work to compensate for them. Ellen spoke of the problems that arose in her household from her mother's unexpected moods and tantrums.

Finally, Ellen said, "You don't come in tomorrow, do you?"

"No," Annie said. "Too bad John doesn't have the same day free."

"Well, I work tomorrow, and must go if I'm to get any sleep. Though it's early, do you want to walk back with me?"

"No," Annie said, sadly. "I'll stay and have another."

"Don't let your sadness drive you to drink. I've seen you having more lately."

"I won't," Annie said.

Once Ellen had gone, she ordered a quartern of rum. Once she'd finished that, she had another. She forgot to eat supper.

~ ~ ~

"Annie, dear," John said. "You must wake up now, and go home."

She opened her eyes to find herself in the mews where John lodged over the Buridge's Hotel stables. Her head ached, and her mouth tasted of spoiled potatoes.

"How did I...?" she asked.

"You were drunk and looking for me," John said.

She could tell that he wanted to be angry. Instead, he had sympathy.

"But I don't remember...."

"Sometimes that happen when one has a lot to drink," he said.

Annie shook her head. She remembered having two, maybe three quarterns of rum. After that, nothing.

John frowned sadly. "Mr. Ward knows about us now. He were going to let me go, yet I spoke with him, told him you were expecting and he's changed his mind. Still, I could lose the position should things not go well. You caused a scandal in the hotel dining room trying to find him and then giving him what for about my hours. He were embarrassed, but he's good man. He even chuckled a bit describing your indignation on my behalf. 'A glorified delver,' he said you called him." John chuckled.

Annie felt the tightness of her face and imagined the horrified look she gave John. She shut her mouth and closed her eyes.

"You do know that his company digs tunnels for the railway."

"Yes," she moaned, the vibration of her voice aggravating her headache.

Unable to imagine walking into the front entrance of Buridge's Hotel, let alone entering the establishment's fine dining room and creating a scene before all the fine ladies and gentlemen patrons, Annie felt a cold, hard lump form in her chest that took her breath away. She experienced a fear of herself she'd not known before. John held her as she gulped air.

"Can you forgive me," she asked once she'd calmed somewhat.

"Might just as well have been me."

"Oh, no," she said, imagining John making a similar scene. In the year they'd known each other, she'd seen him highly intoxicated many times, yet he seemed to become quiet while drunk, as she got louder. "Never that."

"You should go home. Mr. Ward said I might take you in the four wheel trap, if you'd like."

She regretted agreeing to allow him to drive her. The wheels on the cobblestones rattled her head to the point of agony. At the southeast corner of Hyde Park, she said, "Leave me here and I'll walk the rest of the way."

Reluctantly, he stopped the trap, and allowed her to climb down.

"I'll look into getting us a room of our own," he said.

Annie brightened, and she smiled for John. He turned the trap, deftly threading his course between other vehicles, and headed back the way he'd come. Having something to look forward to, Annie felt somewhat better on her walk home. She smiled at strangers moving in the opposite direction, though her aching head kept insisting she retreat from the world.

~ ~ ~

The next day, when Annie got home from work, she found Emily and Mum waiting for her.

"Ellen told us about the scandal you caused at the Buridge's Hotel dining room," Emily said.

Annie bowed her head in shame. Ellen Webster had betrayed her. "She might have talked to me about it first."

"She is merely trying to look out for you," Emily said.

Mum quieted Emily with a look. "Your sister is not likely to listen to you if all you've got are accusations and shaming."

Mum took Annie's hands in her own. "Your father had a terrible thirst." She shook her head sadly. "Perhaps you do as well."

Annie didn't know how to respond. She didn't like to think she was like her father in that regard. She'd hated that in him.

"I'm sorry I spoke to you that way." Emily said. She sat on the bed she still shared with Annie. "Please, I'd like to tell you something." She patted the straw mattress.

Annie settled uneasily beside her, and Mum set about to heat water for tea.

"I have been having trouble with drink," Emily said. "You don't know about it because I was ashamed and hiding it. Once I have a drink I want more and struggle to stop. I have awakened not knowing what I've done, having lost memory of part of a day."

Annie looked her in the eye, surprised to find such an odd link with her sister. They had rarely got along. "That is what happened to me. I don't remember going to the hotel."

"I'm not surprised," Emily said. "We are our father's daughters."

Annie thought of all the times Dadda had forgotten something he'd done, said, or even promised while drunk.

"I signed the teetotalism pledge," Emily said. "I feel so much better doing without."

Annie frowned.

"Come with me to a temperance meeting tonight," Emily said, "just to listen."

Annie's frown deepened. She didn't like religion.

"You don't have to believe what they do," Emily said. "Just listen to the stories."

Mum served tea, and helped to persuade Annie to go and at least listen.

At the meeting that night, the speaker told of his moodiness, his rages, his cruelty to family, and how he'd lost the love of a good woman, all because of drink. Annie found herself painfully reminded of her most unpleasant experiences with her father. She had a moment of panic toward the end of his presentation, and when the call went up for those willing to sign the pledge of abstinence, Annie fell in line and signed.

Emily smiled much of the way home.

Shamefully, Annie wanted a drink.

~ ~ ~

Annie removed from her mother's room in Montpelier Place to live with John in an apartment above stables in Brook's Mews, Bayswater, near Buridge's Hotel. The one chamber, larger than John's previous arrangement and more room than Annie ever had before, had come from his employer in exchange for a cut in John's pay.

Annie continued to work at Price Laundry in Berkeley Street which lay south of her new lodgings and east of those of her mother. Her friendship with Ellen cooled, and eventually became merely business-like.

Although Annie and John were together, Mr. Ward stayed such a busy man, dashing this way and that all over town, she still saw little of her husband. With that, and the fact that her family lived about two miles away, Annie found herself as lonely as ever. Her abstinence didn't last long, not in small part because John continued to drink when in her presence.

Glimpse

After leaving the tun, Annie turned right into Commercial Street, made her way some distance among the foot traffic to Spitalfields Market, and entered at East Street.

Afternoon at the market, the place bustled with activity. Hawkers wore bright clothes, had colorful stalls, wagons, or barrows to attract the eye. They shouted slogans, used noise makers of various sorts or musical instruments to create sounds to draw the ear. The tantalizing smells that rose from carts belonging to vendors of hot foods mingled unevenly with the various odors of unwashed humanity, creating an unsettling mix of desire and disgust. Numerous objects prominently displayed, toys for children and curios for those with dispensable funds, competed for Annie's attention. With the unpleasant overlapping of aromas, the cacophony of sound, and confusion of color and motion irritating her slight hangover, Annie would not linger. She hurried to a woman selling bread from a barrow, and spent a precious farthing on a small slice, spread thinly with butter. Dodging a group of guttersnipes making a flimp-pass through the crowd at the entrance to the market, Annie hurried out the way she'd come in. She gripped her few possessions through the fabric of her skirt to make certain no small hands got into her pocket.

Back out on Commercial Street, she turned right and moved south. Stepping into the crossing at Brushfield Street to reach the other side, Annie realize nearly too late that a growler came straight at her from the right. She whirled around, retreating back onto the footway, and collided with a man. His cap fell from his head and he dropped a sack from off his shoulder. Annie lost her bread, and gripped his coat to keep her feet. He shoved her aside and she fell, her left knee striking the stone pavers. Annie rolled with the pain onto her side, and bit her lip to keep from crying out.

"You a dipper," he asked, standing upright, "trying for my purse, old girl?" The short, sandy-haired fellow checked the pockets of his ill-fitting readymade jacket and trousers. He bent to pick up his fallen cap and the sack, his movement swift and full of disgust.

Annie didn't rise. She kept her eyes on him. "No, sir. An accident, sir."

"You think I have clods for brains?"

He drew back his foot to kick her, then seemed to think better of it as he glanced around at the other pedestrians striding past and watching the scene.

Annie saw his mouth working, no doubt to gather saliva. Although she saw what would come, she was too proud to flinch away from the insult. The same feeling that made her shy away from begging also kept her from protecting herself from the spittle that flew in her face. With her eyes locked on his, he reacted to her steady gaze uneasily. A brief look of shame came over him, and he turned and walked away.

Annie did not get up immediately. She held back tears meant for her father, her children, and herself. Those using the footway walked around her. No one offered assistance. Annie saw her buttered bread beside her and picked it up. She tried to relax against the hard stones.

Did Dadda toughen me up? Either he had, or at some point she'd succeeded in becoming someone else.

She ate her buttered bread, road grit and all.

The tender child I was could never have endured what I do. Indeed, without complaint, she'd allowed a stranger to abuse her on the street; not because she deserved punishment, but because she could not rail at all the abuses heaped against her.

To complain does no good. I am tired of feeling sorry for myself.

Annie stood and considered her surroundings as if for the first time, the hard roads, the hard buildings, the hard traffic, and the hard people. Just as her tongue had found the road grit in her bread, her eyes found the grit and grime, mostly the soot from coal burning, that had settled into every nook and cranny, each crack and crevice in every surface of the landscape. Everything, including most of the pedestrians, appeared to have been rubbed down with shoeblack and then roughly wiped clean.

This is not a good place, she thought. *How have I allowed myself to become accustomed to the pain, the filth, the stench, the…shadows?*

And, quite suddenly, as if in answer to her question, she stepped away from herself.

Filled with a childlike wonder, she was astonished to occupy the failing forty-seven-year-old shell that stumbled around London's East End. The middle-aged woman could not truly be Annie. Her aches and pains fell away.

This is how I felt as a child.

Annie became curious about those on the street. How many children did the woman in the maroon crossover shawl have? The large flat case the man in the bent blue hat carried—what did it hold? Drawings? Maps? Clothing patterns? Designs for a new type of dreadnaught? The woman wearing the worn-out skirt, the old green silk dress bodice, and the black straw bonnet, what had happened to the other half of her spectacles? She squinted at the newspaper she held with an expression of intense concern. What story did she read?

Seeing a man in a bloody apron driving a wagon, possibly a carman who made deliveries to butchers, Annie grew unaccountably afraid. She remembered the cat's meat man from her childhood; his bright clothes, cold eyes, the squeaking wheels of his reeking barrow, and the disgusting green and blue meat he sold.

And, as quickly as the childlike glimpse of the world had come, the vision departed. Thankfully so did the fear. Annie watched the carman turn his wagon into the street at the next corner.

Despite the fear of the cat's meat man, the glimpse had been exciting; a brief remembrance of the possibilities life offered. *A wonderful moment,* she thought, then worried that the strange outlook had somehow been a product of poor diet or lack of sleep.

Even so, she usually walked the streets with little curiosity. Annie saw her reflection in a building's ground floor window across the street—she was smiling.

What has she got to smile about? The question echoed in her head from Wednesday night/Thursday morning, when she'd asked the same thing about the woman who helped her out of the road.

Could it be that, as hard as life had been for the woman, she also experienced some childlike wonder? Perhaps we all carry a bit of the child we were, and owe something to that life.

Ah—that's the girl John wants me to save!

So obvious once she'd thought of it—the little girl inside Annie had helped her become sober the year she stayed in the Asherton House asylum.

I am much *indebted to her.*

The unguarded perspective brought her yet another revelation of debt: *I owe Eliza an apology.*

Childbearing

Annie wanted to have children with John, but more than that, she could see clearly that he wanted to have children. During her first pregnancy, morning sickness warned of greater misery to come. Dreading the agony of childbirth, Annie drank and made little effort to hide her indulgence. John expected her to suffer with the pregnancy, and allowed her to shirk her domestic duties and seek intoxication.

"You should leave off with the drink now as you're pregnant," Mum told her. "You don't want to bear sick children."

"Few women set aside drink whilst knapped." Annie said in a churlish tone. "Children are born with all sorts of illnesses. Who's to say which problems might come from drink?"

Several weeks into her pregnancy, Annie had a miscarriage while alone at home. When she told John, he struggled to maintain a brave face. He wiped a tear away before saying. "Well, I can think of no more pleasant work than making children. We'll just have to keep at it."

~ ~ ~

Mum continued to harp on the idea that drinking was harmful to the unborn, and that persuaded Annie to cut back.

In the seventh month of her second pregnancy, John received word that his favorite cousin, Bertie, a seaman, wanted to come visit. John begged Mr. Ward for an evening off, and left for the docks to fetch his cousin, while Annie prepared a nice fish stew and put their room in order.

She looked forward to showing their new lodgings to the visitor, whom she'd never met. The room had an area of twelve by fourteen feet. The chimney drew well enough above the broad coal grate that the air in the room remained clear. John had bought them a new bed, night stand, and armoire. The table and chairs had been a wedding gift from his parents. She'd made and hung a calico curtain on the room's single window.

The two men arrived sodden with gin and in a raucous good mood. John set two bottles of gin, one half empty, on the table. After an interval of teasing, laughing, and wrestling playfully with one another, the men settled down and John made introductions.

"My wife, Annie," he said, still giggling.

Annie smiled for the two men, gave a tiny curtsy.

Bertie, all smiles, merely nodded. "I'll have more of that gin," he said.

John handed over the half-empty bottle.

Annie wanted to join their fun, and allowed John to pour her a glass of gin. She served the stew and the men said nothing while they ate heartily. Then their talk and laughter resumed.

When she could not find her way into their conversation, she had another glass of gin to soothe her feelings. At the time, she saw consuming that amount of drink as partaking lightly.

As Annie sat listening to the men, a wave of nausea rolled over her. "I'm not feeling well," she told John. Having grown accustomed to her complaints since the pregnancy began, he merely responded with a nod of his head.

The discomfort became so severe that, although embarrassed to do so, she repaired to the bed fully clothed.

Bertie seemed to notice her for the first time. Appearing more embarrassed than Annie, his restless gaze found no comfortable spot in the room to rest. John tried to continue the conversation, yet Bertie clearly didn't listen.

Annie held her swollen belly and rocked gently, trying to soothe herself. She moaned quietly, her nausea, like a gathering storm in her belly, becoming so great she feared she might lose the infant that night.

Bertie interrupted John. "Is the baby coming?" he asked with a look of panic.

John reached over to pat his cousin's shoulder. "She still has a couple more months."

Bertie became somewhat calmer. He smiled uncertainly for John, and turned to Annie. "May I do something to help?" he asked.

"That's kind of you," she said. "Feeling ill isn't unusual whilst knapped. It shall pass like any other storm."

Not entirely put at ease, Bertie blurted, "My mum says rocking like that when she carried me give me good sea legs."

"She knew before you were born as you'd go to sea?" John asked with a doubtful look.

"Of course." Bertie said with a forced bark of a laugh.

He turned back to Annie with a bright look, as if he suddenly realized he had something to say. "I see a sou'wester." he cried, as if needing to be heard over the wind at sea. "Hold fast, little one. She's an old vessel…" He paused to beam at John and jab him in the shoulder. "…but a sound one. You hold fast, and she'll weather the storm." He laughed uneasily.

Annie didn't think him funny. Nor did John by the look on his face.

He asked about his Aunt Hester. Bertie seemed grateful for the change of subject, and spoke about his mother. Within a short time, the two cousins returned to their playful banter.

Annie's nausea increased and she struggled unsuccessfully to remain quiet. A couple of times, her outbursts interrupted the men.

Finally, looking peevish, John turned to her. "Take another daffy of the lush." He stood and poured two fingers of the fiery liquid into her glass.

"No more," Annie said, "Mum says the child will suffer."

"The drink will calm the infant just as it does you." He placed the glass within her reach on the small nightstand, then sat back down in his chair at the table.

After finishing her drink, she was blessed with quieter voices from the men and eventually sleep as well.

Two months later, in 1870, she gave birth to a delicate girl. Annie found herself somewhat astonished that the tiny creature had survived the arduous journey to life. With the years before her marriage to John, in which she'd resigned herself to spinsterhood, and the couple's grief over the miscarriage, her excitement at finally becoming a mother seemed magical, a gift from heaven. For all her fear of the pain of childbirth, once the child had come, Annie couldn't quite recall the agony she knew she'd experienced.

"She looks just like her mother," John said.

Annie didn't think that a good thing.

She felt intense pride the first time the infant focused her eyes on her. Holding the child to her breast for feeding, they seemed to become one, and Annie felt a swelling love. She marveled at the downey hair on the girl's head, and the pink, callous-free flesh of her fingers and toes.

Her large blue eyes and the dimples below the corners of her perfect, pink mouth held Annie's fascination. Plump and warm, smelling of life, the infant deserved to be known by something pretty. Annie decided that Lily would suit the girl nicely. Then, she feared that remembering the child's name in the future would make the loss worse should the girl depart suddenly.

"I shall not give her a name until she's been with us for a month," Annie told her mother.

"Try not to worry, dear," Mum told Annie. "It doesn't do any good."

The child continued to hold on, and Annie gained some hope. When finally the time came to name her, Annie could not remember the one she'd intended to give, so she named her Emily, after her sister. Shortly thereafter, she remembered the name, Lily, and decided that would be a good nickname to help distinguish the child from her sister.

Despite the warm feelings early on, Annie struggled to be a parent, finding the sense of responsibility to her child daunting. She drank to quiet her unease. She had difficulty with responding to Lily's crying, with the grotesque nature of wiping the girl's nose and mouth, and with cleaning up her stool.

As with any other client, Mum accepted payment from John to take care of Lily by day so Annie could work at the laundry. Because of the distance between her home in the mews and her mother's lodgings, most often traveled in the four wheel trap John borrowed from his employer, Annie frequently left her child with her mother over night.

Since Lily is at Mum's all day, Annie told herself, *taking care of her at night too is little extra work.*

~ ~ ~

In the ensuing years, Annie experienced a few periods of memory loss when drinking heavily. Shame prevented her from talking about the problem. When together, she and John got along well as they sought intoxication to smooth over life's rough edges.

A year and a half after the birth of Lily, Annie experienced a stillbirth in the seventh month of her third pregnancy. She struggled to drink less with some success. In 1872, she went to another temperance meeting with Emily and signed the pledge once more. She became pregnant a fourth time and, in 1873, little Annie came into the world. Annie's difficulties with the responsibilities of motherhood intensified.

With Lily, Annie's mother had resisted taking over parenting duties entirely, making an occasional fuss about keeping her over night. With the coming of little Annie, Mum seemed to have a change of heart; she didn't even complain about keeping both children. The reason came clear one Saturday afternoon as Annie and John arrived at her mother's lodgings in the trap to collect the children.

"You're not much of a mother," Mum said. "I know the only reason they're going with you now is that John wants them home tomorrow, a day he doesn't work."

She speaks the truth, Annie thought, feeling small inside. She said nothing in response.

On the way back to the mews in the trap, she tried to quiet her shame. *She would prick my pride to make me a better mother, but she loves her grandchildren, and her household income doesn't suffer. John's payments each week help, and Georgina and Mirium, with their piece work, do too.* She knew that when she got home a drink would soothe the raw feelings.

While delivering the children back to her mother early Monday morning, Annie excused herself to visit the privy. Afterward, entering her mother's room, she caught the tail end of a conversation between Mum and John.

"....should not have any more children," her mother said. With the noise of the children already assembled for the day in Mum's room, Annie missed the first part of the sentence, yet easily figured out what her mother meant.

John noticed Annie listening, and merely nodded his head.

Annie also thought she should have no more children. She didn't discuss the matter with John and didn't know what he thought of Mum's statement until the next day, when he returned to the mews for his supper.

"From now on," he said. "I could wear a sheath when I visit with Lady Laycock." He dramatically opened a waterproof envelope to reveal a gray and white sheep's gut sheath for Annie's inspection. "Should we clean it afterward, we can use it several times."

Although pleased with the idea that they might have sexual relations without creating more children, Annie was skeptical. "Is it knotted at one end?"

"Yes, I think it does have a small knot."

She tried to imagine having the disgusting, slimy thing—part of an animal—inside her. "Won't that feel odd?"

"We can try it."

Annie agreed.

~ ~ ~

Clearly, John saw what Annie had become, and knew she wasn't up to being a mother. Even so, in drunken passion and in too much of a hurry to be bothered, they would dab it up without remembering to use a sheath. Even if they did use one, they sometimes grew so rough in their lovemaking that they tore a hole in the sheep gut. They destroyed three before giving up on the device.

John was a good father when home and not drunk. For the first few years of fatherhood, until Lily was at least six years old and little Annie three, he told his girls wonderful, humorous bedtime stories. Lily in particular loved that enough to openly lament its passing when he began to prefer to drink in the evenings instead. At least her father did not have a cruel streak like Dadda's. Yet, like Annie's father, as time passed, John lost much of his lightheartedness. His sense of humor diminished. He worked longer hours and spent even less time at home.

~ ~ ~

"It's too heavy full of water, Mum," Lily complained.

"It holds none yet," Annie said.

"When it *is* full, Mum."

"You whinge about every little thing. Do as I asked." She'd become determined to toughen the girl up.

Annie turned back to swatting the flies that buzzed around the dirty dishes. The pot, bowls, and utensils had been dirty for too long. She cleaned up only when she had to. The room smelled of rotten food, dirty clothes, and old slops. The children had been at her mother's lodgings for nearly a week, but had returned home the day before. The hot summer air in the mews had made the second floor apartment miserable. Somewhat hungover from drinking with John the past night, Annie had a short temper.

Lily had taken the chamber pot to the privy for dumping. Otherwise, she offered little help cleaning up without being hounded. Little Annie, at age five, was next to worthless. Currently, she napped in the bed.

Annie turned to find that Lily hadn't left to fetch water. She stood in the same spot, a damnable frown fixed around her big brown eyes, as she stared at her mother sadly like some beaten pup.

"What is your age, seven years?" Annie asked. She'd had to subtract the year of the girl's birth from the current year, 1878, to come up with the number.

"Almost eight," Lily said, her forlorn expression deepening.

"When I was your age, I carried a two gallon bucket," Annie said. In truth, she hadn't carried two gallons of water from the public pump until she was twelve years old and then she'd done it with two buckets and a shoulder pole. "You're a weakling. Fetching water will build up your strength. Now, go!"

Lily took up the wooden vessel by the handle. She had to hold it out from her side to keep it from swinging into her legs as she walked to the stairs to go out. Carrying the thing that way, she'd be fatigued by the time she got to the public pump nearly a quarter of a mile away, worn out by the time she got home with it filled.

Annie found herself somehow pleased by the girl's difficulty, then unsettled to realize that she felt that way. Still, she'd become weary of the child's inability to help out, and so her hardheartedness seemed justified.

When Lily returned, slicked with sweat and with a bucket half-filled, Annie said, "Why, you are a glocky shirkster, aren't you?" The tipple of gin she'd had while the girl was gone loosened her tongue.

"But Mum, I tripped when halfway home and spilled some." Lily seemed on the verge of tears.

Annie took the bucket and poured the water from it into the basin on the cupboard. Then, as Lily watched, her woeful expression an infuriating thing to look upon, Annie got a knife from the cupboard and used it to make a mark on the inside of the bucket, two inches from the top.

"Out you go, to fetch more water," Annie said. "When you get home, the bucket better be full to that mark."

Lily picked up the bucket and put it on her head, perhaps to help hide her crying, and went out.

Annie had another tipple before washing the dishes.

Again, Lily returned slicked with sweat. She proudly showed her mother the water in the bucket.

"That's half an inch too little," Annie said, pointing to the mark she'd made in the wood of the vessel.

"I-I stumbled again, and lost but a little," Lily said, offering a forced smile.

"It's not enough. I ought send you back out."

Lily began to cry again.

"Weepy little wretch!" Annie sang. "Cannot walk and fetch!"

Lily sat on the floor, covered her head with her thin arms, and sobbed. Annie found delight in the child's suffering.

Why would I be pleased to see my beautiful girl so unhappy?

She realized that she'd been increasingly hard on Lily for some time, perhaps a year or more. Annie did not understand why she acted that way. Realizing that her father had at times seemed confounded by his own cruelty, Annie unexpectedly saw herself in the girl. Her eyes stung as tears rose up.

Although she knew she should apologize for mistreating Lily, pride wouldn't allow such an admission of wrongdoing. Even so, Annie had to end the torment. She crouched down in front of her daughter. "We have plenty of water," she said softly. She stroked the girl's head until Lily stopped crying and looked up uncertainly. "I won't send you back out if you'll help me finish cleaning up."

Lily forced another smile, got up, and helped out.

~ ~ ~

Despite Annie's dismay over the incident, her mistreatment of her eldest daughter continued on and off as time went on. She didn't talk to anyone about the problem until 1879.

"I call Lily names," she confided to her sister, Emily.

They sat at her mother's place, having tea and waiting for Mum to get home.

"I shout at the poor girl. Should she do something different from the way I might do it, I belittle her."

"Reminds me of how Dada treated you," Emily said. "Is she your *favorite?*"

Rage boiled up. Annie turned and slapped Emily, then felt terrible. Her sister didn't flinch away.

"I'm sorry," Annie said.

Emily looked at her in silence. Her question had stirred Annie's sense of herself—not because Lily received favor, but because it put Annie in a position of making an uncomfortable comparison. She'd seen herself in the suffering Lily, yet until the present moment had resisted comparing herself to her father. She found making the measure frightening.

"I knew I had to talk about it when I started to do the same to little Annie. Something about treating another girl named Annie that way gave me a chill. I don't want to be our father."

"Perhaps you feel the chill of Dadda's grave," Emily said.

The words brought forth tears, and Annie wept as she leaned into her sister's shoulder. Emily held her silently.

Mum came in, asked, "What's this all about?"

Her daughters sat up straight.

"Annie is ready to go to another temperance meeting," Emily said. "There's one Thursday night."

~ ~ ~

The third signing of the pledge did little good. Annie didn't want to see the connection between her tippling and her cruelty to her girls. Because drinking had become so important and she didn't want to see herself mistreating her children, having them around less solved her problem.

On the few occasions she became sober, an increasingly rare state in recent years, Annie tried to express her love for her children. She did feel affection for them, but not often enough to keep their needs in mind.

She kept telling herself that a moment would come in which she would shed her destructive ways and be a better mother and wife. That moment often seemed to be around the corner, just beyond one more deep dip in the lush.

~ ~ ~

In 1880, following three more miscarriages, and an additional stillbirth, poor, crippled John came into the world, his legs paralyzed.

Annie knew that Mum had been right to ask her to stay away from drink while pregnant, yet she could not stop herself.

When sober enough to consider her losses, Annie's most charitable thoughts toward herself were that she'd put her unborn at risk. In truth, she knew that she'd murdered several of her own children and maimed one.

~ ~ ~

In 1882, at the age of twelve, an infection of the brain took Lily's life. Annie knew she had been a deplorable mother to the girl.

Guilt and regret piled one atop the other, and she needed help to keep from feeling the loss. Her drinking increased.

Family

Still hungry after eating her bread with butter and road grit, Annie returned to Spitalfields Market, and spent a ha'penny on a large potato. She walked to Crossingham's, thinking that if she got into the kitchen and spent time there, Eliza would eventually turn up. Then, Annie would have the opportunity to offer her apology.

"Come to return your key, Dark Annie?" Timothy Donovan asked in greeting as she stepped into his office.

"No, Tim," Annie said. "I don't have it just now. I will return the key soon or pay for my room in whole. May I cook my potato in the kitchen?"

"You may sit in the kitchen," Mr. Donovan said, "but you don't have a room, so you can't cook. You've been a good lodger, or I'd have to do something about the missing key. Return it by tomorrow and I won't charge you extra."

Annie smiled for him. "Is number 29 still available?"

"Yes."

She turned toward the stairs to go down to the kitchen.

"Where have you been all week?" Donovan asked.

"The Infirmary," she said without pausing. Admitting that she'd slept rough much of the week would have been shameful.

Eliza wasn't in the kitchen. Possibly she would come in if Annie stayed for a while. She sat at one of the tables, eating her potato raw and trying to decide how to gain funds. She needed four pence to stay in a doss house, eight pence if she wanted to get back into number 29. The latter remained unlikely. She tried to persuade herself to go to family and beg for money.

None of them liked her. She reminded Mum and Emily of what they'd hated in Dadda. Annie's younger siblings, Georgina, Mirium, and

Fountain, having had little chance to know Dadda were merely disgusted with Annie for her history of drinking.

Even her namesake had looked at her with contempt when Annie last visited her mother.

I deserve no better.

Little Annie had reached fifteen years of age. She lived with Mum. A hard worker, the girl had become invaluable to Annie's mother in making ends meet.

In recent memory, seven-year-old little John was the only one of her family to offer Annie a smile during one of her visits. In July, Mum had been relieved of the burden of little John, having found a home for him at the Crippled Boys National Industrial Home, Woolsthorpe House, in Wright's Lane, Kensington.

And there's my thanks to the lad. For all the long title memorized, even the address, I can't be bothered to remember if he trained in relief stamping or copper plate printing. Damn my bloody memory.

If her father had been alive, little John might have apprenticed with him and become a cobbler or shoemaker. Annie's life had suffered many a bad turn since her father took his own life. At times, she wanted to blame him for the hardship, her drinking, and her family's hardened hearts, but, though she remained angry with him, she loved him still. Her sense of responsibility for his death only complicated her feelings further.

After at least half an hour of waiting with the hope that Eliza might come in, Annie decided that sitting in the kitchen did little good. She would happen upon the woman eventually.

As she left Crossingham's and emerged into the golden, late afternoon light, Annie saw Amelia Palmer headed for the lodging house.

Her friend paused to talk. "How are you getting on?"

Annie couldn't tell Amelia that she'd been sleeping rough. "I have been too ill to earn anything, and have lost my room."

"You'll be needing to return this, then." Amelia gave her back the key to number 29.

"I'm trying to pull myself together to find some money so I can go to a doss house," Annie said.

"Do you have any lace or yarn products to hawk at Stratford Market this evening?"

"No, not tonight."

"Do you need your accoutrements so you can make some?"

"Not enough time. Nowhere to set up. I know they're safe with you."

"I'd give you something to help, but I spent my last on a meager supper that waits in my room."

"Not to worry," Annie said. "I'll think of something."

Once Amelia had moved on, Annie returned the key to Mr. Donovan, then stood out front of Crossingham's looking at the orange, late afternoon sunlight that illuminated the tops of the buildings along Commercial Street to the east. The warm light diminished and the structures returned to their somber colors as she again considered going to family and asking for money.

Possibly because of her family's bitterness toward her, she had no compunction about begging them for funds. Two weeks earlier, she'd run into her brother, Fountain, in Commercial Street.

"Annie," he said.

He clearly did not want to talk to her, and might have past her by without speaking if he hadn't seen that she saw him. All her family acted that way whenever they met her on the street. Though she knew she'd grievously wronged her children and expected nothing from them, she believed her siblings, especially the three youngest, owed her gratitude.

Annie hid her anger, said, "I'm hard up. I need money for my lodgings. Can you help?"

He frowned.

"If not for me toiling so hard when you were young," she said sharply, "you would have worked instead of going to school. You can read—that's because of me."

"And Mum... and Em," he added.

"Yes, Mum and Emily too."

He frowned again, shoved his hand in his pocket, and fished out a couple of coins.

"Two shillings?" She said.

"That's all I've got."

He handed the money over and they parted without another word. She'd spent much of the money on drink.

Would that that had happened tonight. I'd have enough for number 29, and a good lush.

So late in the day, she didn't have time to go to her mother in Brompton.

Emily lived in Vauxhall. Yes, she might easily ask Emily for money, but even Vauxhall was a long way to walk starting so late, and by chance, she might not be there. Annie didn't want to make the effort for naught.

Amelia appeared on the street again. "You're still here," she said.

"Yes, there's no use going all that way," Annie said as if Amelia had known about her thoughts of going to her sister. "I'll have to look elsewhere for the money to pay for my lodgings."

Amelia looked somewhat confused. She also seemed in a hurry. "I'm off to meet Henry. I haven't seen him in most of a week."

She is lucky to have a husband to love, Annie thought as her friend walked away.

Discouraged about her prospects for the night ahead and needing something to lift her spirits, Annie tried for another of those crisp glimpses of the world through younger eyes, and found that she couldn't accomplish the childlike outlook on command.

John had as much as told Annie she should continue to live for the sake of the girl inside her.

He's dead, though, and perhaps the child is as well.

Surely with all the miscarriages and stillbirths, the child within me died too.

Was the girl indeed long gone, her remains merely a ghostly wistfulness for better times?

Annie hugged herself to ward off a dreadful chill that came with the notion that she haunted herself.

No, Annie decided, *she isn't gone. I can still feel the life of the girl. I remember.*

Years ago, while at the Asherton House asylum, she'd tried to have a conversation with the girl. She'd asked, *How have we been separated?*

Then, as now, no good answer came.

Is she too fragile or proud to bide with me in this grim world?

Dadda did *toughen me up.*

Was that a good thing?

Had he driven the girl into hiding, only to be coaxed out with John's charm and wit? Even then, the moments when Annie had felt such childlike abandon with her husband dimmed over time and became infrequent.

The momentary glimpse earlier that day had been wonderful, but so short-lived.

And John would have me continue for that?

Annie would be the girl again if she could; the innocent and good child with the full and whole heart, unsullied by inhuman compromise. That would be something beautiful. Yet the child would never survive the East End on her own.

Surely, I have more to live for than that.

She felt a growing chill in the air. Delicate dusk had effortlessly edged out the daylight to make way for its colder, overshadowing master. With the gathering gloom, Annie set out to find a client.

Out

"I have lost my position, Annie," John said. He sat on the edge of the bed with his head in his hands. Something sharp about his smell told her he'd just come in from outside.

She'd awakened with a pounding headache and a taste of rot in her mouth. As she tried to roll over on the straw mattress, she ached and her stomach churned with nausea.

John had been gone for some time, how long uncertain. She'd done little since he left but drink.

He's sad because he lost something.

"Don't be sad," Annie said. The words resonated inside her mouth and throat in a way that hurt.

John glanced at her nearly in tears, looking as if he'd wept earlier.

Annie remembered that the children, including little John, were with Mum.

She made the great effort of sitting up and reaching to caress his shoulder. He didn't wear his livery. Midday light came through the window. To which day of the week the light belonged, Annie could not have said.

"This time, you caught him strolling in Hyde Park," John said.

"Who?" she asked.

"Mr. Ward."

"I've been nowhere," she said, indignant. Remembering her past periods of forgetfulness, though, fear welled up inside her.

"You cursed him," John said, "and said that he kept me from you. You blamed him for little John being born a cripple. He tried to get away. You clung to his coat, and finally his leg. I saw him trying to get away, and ran to help. You *bit* his leg!"

Annie couldn't remember any of that. He might have been telling her of an event on the other side of the world for all that she could picture the happenings. Still, without that he pursued a jest, he wasn't the lying sort, and nothing in his expression spoke of good humor. What he said must be true, and she'd been the disgraceful fool to bring the harm.

Annie tumbled out of bed, her head throbbing, and vomited into the basin.

"I have destroyed us!" she said, sitting on the floor and gasping for breath.

"No," John said, finally looking her in the eye. "If you were all of it, he would not have let me go. He'd spoken to me several times about having a hangover while on duty. I have even driven for him still in the lush from the night before. He always knew."

"I'm sorry, John," Annie said. She got up to try to hold him, but he held her off.

"You are not yourself," he said. "And you smell like death."

She huddled on the floor and wept. Annie feared herself, and wanted out of the life she'd made. She would start over if possible, and if she could take John with her.

"All that were a week ago," he said.

"No, that doesn't make sense. I haven't been alone that long." As she had done during other benders, Annie tried to gauge the passage of time with memories of how many times she got up to use the chamber pot. She saw that the porcelain vessel under the bed held little. She did recall that at least once, unwilling to use the stairs to take the pot to dump in the privy, she'd slid the window sash up and dumped the slops into the street below, an act that could draw a significant fine. If she had indeed been intoxicated for a week, she suspected she'd committed the unlawful act numerous times.

"Your mother looked in on you for me," John said. "On her first visit, you two spoke of your father. You slept for days thereafter, she said."

"I don't remember," Annie said. How could she not recall a conversation like that?

"I'm not surprised with the amount of lush you've had." He shook his head. "Mr. Ward gave me a reference, and I have found a new position as a valet, one in which I must not be seen to drink. We shall go to live in Windsor. Your mum has agreed to keep the children until we're settled."

A change! Annie felt her sore eyes widen a bit. *Will I indeed get to* make a new life with John?

As more questions began to form, she noticed he seemed troubled. He looked her in the eyes, his gaze penetrating, and said, "You must give up drink."

What had begun to seem hopeful, turned abruptly dark and foreboding, yet with the horror of having cost John his livelihood, and a fear of losing him, Annie turned again to look at her drinking. Although she hated losing control of herself when intoxicated, she loved the feeling as the hard edges of the world were blunted.

She knew John could see the distress in her eyes. "You must try," he said, a tear falling down his cheek.

"Yes," Annie said unsteadily. She had serious doubt that she could survive without.

"I shall abstain as well," he said, "and we'll get through this together. We begin *now*, as we make preparations to remove to Windsor."

Annie swallowed hard. She gripped John's hands and smiled for him, then tried to ignore her cravings as they began the work of packing up their belongings.

Despite her best efforts, Annie quickly demonstrated that she would be of no help. She excused herself repeatedly to wretch in the basin, to evacuate the runny fecal matter from her bowel into the chamber pot, or to simply lie in the bed, writhing against the cramps in her belly.

"Just a daffy," she said to John, "to ease the pain."

She grew hopeful as he stopped loading a trunk he'd borrowed from Mum and fetched the bottle of gin from the cupboard. The roughly one third of a quart in the bottle represented the only alcohol within the household. He seemed to consider the lush for a moment. She could tell he wanted a drink too.

He did not take one, nor did he offer the bottle to Annie. Instead, he strode to the basin, and poured the gin into her vomitus.

"No," Annie said, rising too late to stop him.

Seeing her coming toward him, he held out a hand to ward her off. Perhaps he could see that she would drink the gin anyway because he quickly pulled the chamber pot out from under the bed, lifted the basin and dumped the contents into the runny stool in the pot.

Annie watched as the liquids did not mix thoroughly. Her eyes widened as she imagined that, given the chance, she might still pour off some potent gin for herself.

Again, John must have seen her intention. "I must step out to the privy," he said, casually. He took up the chamber pot and headed down the stairs to the mews's back door.

Annie gasped and fell back onto the bed, terrified to realize she was stuck with herself.

John returned from the privy to find Annie in the throes of severe tremors. "You brought me here for cruel. You took my family and me away my desire to be a mother."

To hear them, her words didn't make sense, but he should know what she meant. She continued to rage at him until Dadda took his place. Then, he was to be feared. She cowered in the corner by the bed. Her bowels let loose and she scurried out on all fours to escape the worms that oozed from her backside. She screamed and John tried to grasp and hold her. She beat on his chest and he backed off.

"I must get out," she said, and heard herself repeating the words over and over as she looked about the room for the quickest exit.

John blocked her way to the stairs.

"I must get out, I must get out, I must get out, I must get out." She made for the window. Before she could leap through the closed sash, he seized her and dragged her to the floor.

Annie's heartbeat ran like the steam engine at the laundry on open throttle. Dizzy, she gasped for breath. Sweat poured from her, oozing away in little worms from every part of her body. They crawled out of her clothing and swarmed over John. He held her heedless of the army attacking and eating him. They chewed away his ears, his scalp and lips. They burrowed into his eye sockets and came out his nose.

"Annie!" he said, as half his face disappeared and the worms fell from holes in his cheek and throat.

The light from the window flickered and pulsed. Annie felt her body bucking against John's.

The room dimmed around her.

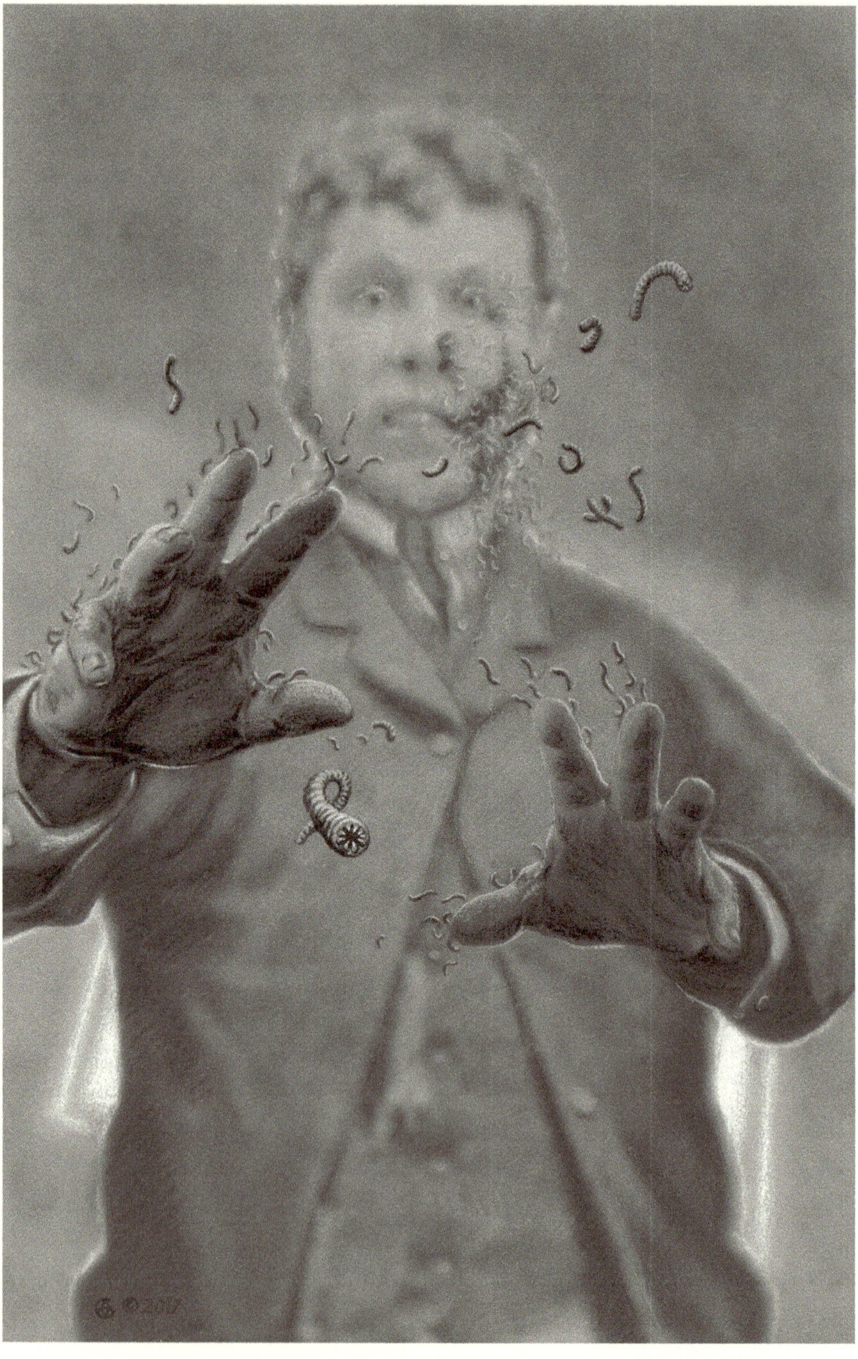

Sherbet

About half past nine o'clock at night, Annie found a client, a cellarman for several local pubs, to pay her tuppence for a romp behind a privy in Miller's Court, off Dorset Street. He agreed with her that they should conduct their business silently. The gas lamp within the L-shaped corridor illuminated the tight area brightly since the walls of each of the buildings surrounding the court had been whitewashed up to the beginnings of the second floors. Consequently, the shadow behind the privy wasn't particularly dark. The privy provided concealment from anyone standing within the court, but if one looked out of a window in the court's southeastern building, Annie and her client might be seen. Curtains fell across each ground-floor window, yet she saw through the glass of the one closest to the court's exit a gap where the fabric sloped out of the way down near the sill to reveal only blackness within. As Annie allowed her client to find his pleasure, she imagined someone crouched on the floor inside the room, looking out through the gap and watching her.

Although unlikely that anyone remained in the darkened room without sleeping, Annie got a chill thinking about the possible presence, and needed escape from a growing fear.

The girl of fancy within her took Annie on an imaginary walk to Vauxhall to beg her sister for money. The best part of the trek was their walk across London Bridge where a street vendor gave them sherbet. Somehow, the frozen, pink treat lasted all the way to Vauxhall.

Once her client had paid and left her, in Annie's mind, the money became what Emily had given her upon her visit to Vauxhall. Her fears of a voyeur aside, the whole experience had been rather painless. Still, she hurriedly left the claustrophobic confines of Miller's Court and the ghostly presence she'd conjured behind the hole in the glass.

The girl saved me from myself. I like her. Perhaps John's right. I need one more client to have my doss.

Asylum

When Annie found herself again, she could not focus her senses well enough to discern her whereabouts. What sights, sounds, and smells came to her were unfamiliar. Later, she would find out that she'd been taken to the Asherton House asylum in Asherton Blight, Wiltshire, nearly one hundred miles from home.

At first, in a slow, boggy panic of realization that she was not home, she wanted to escape. She felt canvas straps binding her to a bed, not so tightly as to cause pain, but well enough to thwart the demand of her sweating, burning, itching skin to be rubbed and soothed. That and the twitching of her muscles became maddening. Despite a sense that others occupied the same white room, her inability to focus her eyes and ears frustrated her efforts to make a determination.

A blurry figure approached, a nurse possibly, and released the straps without a word. The person immediately turned to other duties.

Annie discovered that she wore a gray cotton gown, and what felt like a large nappy, fouled with fluid. She tried to get out of the bed. In her dazed state, she found herself incapable of much action or communication. Her surroundings still made little impression on her. Annie writhed in her bed and ran her hands awkwardly over her body, trying to reach and soothe all the most distressed parts of her skin. The worst burn came from her crotch, under the damp nappy. She reached desperately for patience. Though wanting to remain silent, she moaned in frustration.

The nurse returned with a piece of furniture, a cart perhaps. In Annie's vision, the woman's shape had a bit more definition. The nurse removed the damp cloth, spread a lotion on Annie's sore backside, and applied a fresh nappy. A bowl of something lumpy and gray, and a spoon came into view. At that moment, Annie felt hunger pangs more powerful than any she'd known before. She tried to take the bowl and spoon, but the nurse easily fended off her flailing.

Finally the nurse leaned close and Annie could see her eyes somewhat. "You cannot control your movements well enough," the woman said. "If you'll allow me, I'll feed you."

Annie nodded, and was spoon-fed the gray porridge. While she'd rarely tasted anything so vile, she had never experienced such relish in eating before.

Trying to speak to the woman, she found that she couldn't control her voice well enough and gave up in frustration.

"I am Nurse Atkins," the woman said. "You have been asleep for several days. Soon, your body will begin to feel better. Your mind is another matter. I suggest you listen carefully to Doctor Provensett's lecture."

Once done with her meal, Annie found sleep for a time.

~ ~ ~

When she awoke, Annie found herself more capable of focussing her mind and her senses. The white room held three other beds, two occupied by restless figures restrained with canvas straps. Nurse Atkins helped her into a wicker bath chair and wheeled her to a long, high ward that held about thirty beds. The walls, woodwork, and furnishings had a fresh coat of glossy white paint. Most of the beds' occupants were middle-aged women. Their voices created an overlapping murmur, punctuated occasionally with a shrill cry expressing pain, anger, or delight. Annie gathered no meaning from anything she heard.

Nurse Atkins, with the help of another woman wearing a similar uniform, lifted Annie into a warm bed.

"I suggest you try for more sleep," the nurse said.

Annie would later learn that the others in the ward also had trouble with alcohol. Despite their combined moaning, weeping, and mumbling; despite the rash on Annie's backside, the discomfort in her gut, and the twitching of her muscles, she slept well enough that she awoke several times to see that the light coming through the tall windows of the ward had changed significantly.

On her second day of wakefulness, Nurse Atkins brought Annie a gray uniform to wear. She saw that her name had been stitched onto an inside seam of each piece of clothing, including the bonnet. The nurse also gave her a letter from John. His words were a welcome reassurance that he still loved her and looked out for her wellbeing.

Dearest Annie
I am in Windsor and getting on fine with my new Employer. He is a fusy man but not unreesnable. I have little to drink and only when not on duty.

I must apologies for your rough treetment. There were no other way. I had to tie you in the blanket or I could not save you. If you remember the way you were held with leather cinches don't hold it again the nurses at the infirmry. They were good to you at Saint Gile's and Saint George's Workhouse. You did not sit up without raving and thrashing. When they said you might die I thought I must as well. I visited each day. Slowly your sickness lifted. Although you spoke to me the nurses said you wouldn't remember. They needed your bed and could help no more without sending you to asylum that takes in from the workhouse. I asked if you would go there willingly and you said yes but as they said you may not remember. If not please don't be angry with me. They tell me Asherton House is good for those who drink too much. Don't be frightened love. Your Mum keeps the children safe. We shall all be back together soon.
John

His letter helped fill in some of what remained beyond recollection, and prompted a few more memories to emerge over time.

The slow misery of Annie's gut calmed and the movement of her bowel became more regular within a week. The sweats, the twitching of her muscles, and the poor coordination of her limbs persisted a bit longer.

At the beginning of her second week, a different nurse roused Annie from sleep in the early morning. Flaxen-haired, plump and fair, the woman's skin appeared particularly pink against the neutral colors of her uniform. "I am Nurse Ahern," she said. "You are to attend Doctor Provensett's lecture, then begin to earn your keep in the Women's Dayroom 1."

Annie got up on wobbly legs and followed her to a hall where numerous women assembled to sit in chairs facing a broad window. She sat next to a woman about her age, with thinning salt and pepper hair, a long face, and an extra hole in the side of her nose. Annie had some difficulty looking at her as she could see exposed tissue inside the woman's left nostril.

"I'm Prudy," she said. "And you are?"

"Annie."

"Good to meet you. Would that it were in a pub."

Annie found the suggestion uncomfortable. She'd begun to think that being at the asylum was for the best. Alcohol had seriously frightened her. Although she continued to crave drink, the place didn't have any, and she considered that a good thing. She'd been given small doses of laudanum to help keep her calm.

Annie looked about the room.

Prudy must have seen the question in her eyes. "The doctor will lecture on the virtues of abstinence," she said. "He'll preach self-control, thrift, and self-denial as what makes for good Christians. He'll say as seeking pleasure and leisure is sloth, and that indulging in drink is a form of gluttony, when better food can be had."

Annie had only the most rudimentary religious beliefs, sufficient to believe that life didn't end with death. The rest of Christian faith remained a mystery to her. When asked why the family didn't go to church on Sundays, Dadda had said, "We can't afford it." Mum had never expressed an opinion.

"He thinks as we're gulpy," Prudy said, "He'll say, since we are women from the lowest stations, spending any money of the little we make on drink is theft of earnings needed for our children. He'll say, should we want to better ourselves and rise out of poverty, we will give up drink and devote our bodies and minds to hard work."

She squinted at Annie with a knowing smile. The expression widened the gap in the woman's nostril so that Annie could see the short hairs inside. Out of respect, she kept herself from turning away in disgust.

"As if those of the lower stations don't work hard!" Prudy said. "I've worked fourteen hours a day, six days a week at a cotton mill since I were seven years old. What does he know of hard work? His notion is we are poor because we drink. Well, if you've not walked in my shoes…" she gave a smirk. "Since the inmates here are separated by class, I wonder how his arguments run for those of a higher station."

Prudy paused for a moment before adding, "A word of advice—if you had visions while deep in the lush, keep them to yourself, unless you want to end up in a lunatic asylum."

Annie thought of the worms that had oozed out of her and eaten half of John before she'd become insensible. She'd thought that a dream. With Prudy's talk of visions, she remembered that at the time she'd believed her eyes. Annie nodded to show she understood.

The Doctor entered the room, stood before the great window and delivered a lecture Annie would hear from him in various forms once a week for the next year. He had a pale and slightly yellowed complexion. With white hair and beard, hooded eyes, and a long nose, he might have made a good beak, yet his attire—a checked blue and green suit with black silk waistcoat—belonged to anything but a magistrate.

As he rambled on dryly, Annie turned her attention to the beautiful early autumn day outside the window. The trees still had their green leaves. A wind blew through them, moving branches and rustling leaves that seemed to flash white and green. After a time, she realized that the underside of each leaf was pale and only the top sides green, a bright shade of the color. She'd rarely taken the time to consider trees in London, and they'd never looked quite so good. By comparison to the trees outside the window, the trees in the city looked sickly and dirty.

Prudy had summed up the lecture well. Annie supposed that the woman's disgust arose mainly from the fact that he didn't distinguish between the poor who had problems with drink and those of the poor who didn't. Doctor Provensett clearly believed that all of the lower classes should abstain from drink. Since the majority of his arguments revolved around issues of responsible earning to support family, Annie began to wonder if the doctor thought all of the middle class and wealthy should abstain as well, or if he distinguished between those with an alcohol problem and those who did not have one. Possibly he thought that since the upper classes could afford drink and didn't have to work so hard, indulging wasn't such a problem for them. She didn't get a chance to ask. The staff demanded strict silence from the inmates in the doctor's presence.

Following that first lecture, Nurse Ahern led Annie, along with several other women, to Women's Dayroom 1, to begin her first day of work. The bright room had broad windows so high on the walls that only sky could be seen through them. Work stations, tables and chairs for twenty women stood in rows on the floor. Shelves and tables along two walls held great spools of various yarns in many different colors, baskets that held skeins, needles, hooks, scissors, measuring tapes, bobbins, and booklets of patterns. In one corner stood a weasel for measuring lengths of yarn.

"Our agreement with your husband includes your labor for ten hours each day," Nurse Ahern told her.

Women walked around them and took their places at the work stations.

"You shall begin here with crocheted shawls," she continued. "Should you show ability in the next month or two, our lace-mistress will have you in Rooms 2 for lace-making, and 3 for tatting. Having skills in those pursuits is a value. Inmates in those rooms work only eight hours per day."

Annie excelled at all the various tasks and learned everything she could about knitting, crocheting, lace-making, and tatting.

She settled into life at Asherton House. The food was adequate and her bed warm. Little of what anyone said or did in the asylum helped Annie with her alcohol problem. The place did represent asylum, though, and while she wasn't always treated with respect, she felt safe from the world outside, one in which drink remained available.

When she'd been at Asherton House for a month, she appeared before the superintendent, Mr. Percival Provensett, the doctor's brother. Short, dark, and plump, he looked nothing like his brother. "For our services thus far, you are obliged to give us three months of labor. After that you will be free to go. You may stay longer if you wish, as long as you are willing to provide the labor."

"Thank you sir," Annie said. "I shall gladly give my service. As I near the end of that time, I'll consider how I am faring before deciding whether to stay on or go."

~ ~ ~

Nine months into her stay at the asylum, Annie began to have dreams in which she met with herself as a child. The girl clearly wanted something from Annie, yet could not seem to communicate with words. She found the encounters mysterious and uncomfortable. As she went about her daily work with yarn and thread, hook, needle, and bobbins, Annie thought a lot about the tender girl she'd been. She tried to visit with her while awake, and as she drifted off to sleep at night, to dispel some of the discomfort she felt upon seeing her young self in dreams. Within fancy, she asked questions and tried to determine her younger self's possible answers since the girl did not communicate with words.

How did we become separated?

Perhaps Annie had shoved her aside to get along in a world full of the disgusting, the demeaning, and the frightful.

Yes, she decided that she had.

Where did you go?

No good answer to the question presented itself.

Why can't you speak?

Annie suspected that she had somehow gagged the girl to prevent her from showing outrage. Alternately, she wondered if the child refused to speak out of anger.

Did you leave me?

That seemed more likely.

I could not fault her for being angry.

Instead of protecting the child within, Annie had taken to drinking, which helped her endure the hardships of life. Annie had betrayed herself—at least that part of herself—and exposed the child to increasing torment.

Are you who I was before I drank, or before Dadda died?

Yes, the girl seemed young enough for either to be true.

In Annie's tenth month in the asylum, she asked the girl, *Can you help me to be a better person, a sober wife and mother?*

The girl had a somewhat hopeful look about her, unlike the world-weary and disenchanted face Annie saw in the mirror. Something sustaining sparked behind the child's eyes.

Yet those are my eyes, Annie thought. *Perhaps I do still have hope.*

What if I apologized?

The suggestion left Annie feeling foolish, but that night, in dreams, she found herself expressing her regrets to the girl—including, strangely, for not having thanked Dadda for his gift on the day he died—and begging the child's forgiveness. When Annie awoke, the words she'd used to express herself eluded her. She did remember the girl's smile, though.

Within a day, she noted that her craving for drink had fallen away. She waited a month to see if she still had no desire, then wrote to John and told him of the change.

A month later, in late September of 1884 John came to collect her at the asylum in a fine summer carriage and four that he'd borrowed. He arrived too late for them to set out again that day.

Annie tried to hold back intense emotion during their reunion. The asylum allowed the couple to meet for a few minutes in a small chamber off the entrance foyer to the great house before they were separated for the night. Despite the presence of the asylum porter, watching from the doorway, John lifted Annie from the floor in a deep and loving embrace, and kissed her.

The porter cleared his throat to remind John of his presence. "You have requested accommodation for the night?" the porter asked.

"Yes, so my horses may rest, drink, and feed," John said.

"We can allow you the loft above the stables," the porter said. "The night shouldn't be too chill."

"Thank you, sir."

"Come with me, then." the porter said to John, then he turned to Annie. "You shall see him again in the morning."

Annie slept little that night.

~ ~ ~

"You ought to ride in comfort inside," John said as they prepared to set out for Windsor the next day.

"I'd rather sit with my husband in the driver's box," she said, grinning.

The trip took three beautiful days. Aside from her stay in the asylum, Annie had rarely been out of London and knew little of the countryside. The whole world seemed fresh and new. The sky shown a bright blue like none she'd seen before. At times, her zest for the crisp clear air, the smells of vegetation, the cooling breezes, the light, clean rain, and vistas of the countryside as seen from heights along the road startled her. How had she not noticed the beauties of life before?

They stayed nights, along their journey, at taverns on the road. John made sure the horses would be well-treated before joining Annie for meals and rest. The couple ate well and, in each tavern, they bedded in a private room.

"My monthly flow has not visited since before I went to Asherton House," Annie told John on the first night. They lay together, warm and comfortable, in bed. "I should no longer become knapped."

She'd been concerned that he might be disappointed, but he smiled. Annie laughed as he drew her close. She made love to her John repeatedly that night and the two nights that followed. She "rode" as John liked to say, since she preferred to be on top. Fresh as the experience was, she realized that she wasn't at all certain she'd ever made love to him while sober.

When they finally arrived at a small stone cottage in Windsor, though happy, Annie complained, "I ache between the legs."

"From both rides," John said, and she smiled.

Between Rounds

Annie made the rounds of several pubs, looking for a client or for anyone willing to buy her a drink. She had no success and thought again about trying to find Eliza. As Annie returned to Crossingham's to look for the woman, she found herself close to the warehouse in Commercial Street behind which she'd found the tun. She checked the alley to see if the giant barrel remained. Unfortunately, it had been removed.

She heard the bells for half-past eleven o'clock as she arrived at Crossingham's and approached the nightwatchman, Mr. Evans. "May I rest my feet in the Kitchen?" she asked. "I've been to my sister in Vauxhall to get some money. Need just a bit more." That wasn't quite a lie. Even so, she had no real hope of securing enough funds to get back into number 29.

"For a short time," he said. "One of the stoves is still warm from cooking. Enjoy that for a while, then out you go until you can pay."

She wanted to say that if he saw Eliza, he should tell her that Annie was looking for her. Since she didn't want to explain why, she thought the message might sound a bit like a threat. She imagined Eliza coming at her because she thought that Annie spoiled for a fight, and decided against saying anything about the matter.

She sat in the kitchen, soaking up the warmth and hoping Eliza would turn up. Although each of the large, stained and pitted tables held a lit lamp, the room seemed somber and dreary. Where were the other lodgers? Usually, they gathered in the kitchen to relax and have conversations. Not that Annie had much of anything to say, yet she thought in that moment the murmur of voices would be a comfort. With the silence, she couldn't help considering herself.

Annie felt foolish for putting stock in the idea that she had inside her a small girl that might make life better somehow.

Years ago, I believed that she helped me to give up drink. But how long did abstinence last?

She heard footsteps on the stairs leading down to the kitchen, and looked up, both hoping and dreading to see Eliza.

Frederick Simons entered with a pail of beer that held at least a quart and a half of liquid. She'd known him as a fellow lodger at Crossingham's for over a year. He had a head of dark, curly hair, and a droop to the left side of his mouth.

"Have you seen Eliza," Annie asked.

"No," he said, taking a seat at the other table. He took a gulp from his pail, wiped his mouth on his shirt sleeve. "Got this for tuppence at the Blue Boy." He had the smile of a man who thought he had made a good bargain. "Got a bit of water in it—as what they said—a spill of some sort. Drank one whole pail while I were there. Couldn't carry anymore away with me."

The Blue Boy stood next door to Crossingham's. The place was of the worst sort, serving mostly the gulpy and down and out. Annie had heard that the cook used the castoffs from the glue factories, what even the cat's meat man couldn't sell, for the meat in the Blue Boy's stews. Their mild drink consistently got watered, not just when "a spill of some sort" occurred. Their strong drink often held some quantity of industrial or medical alcohol. The latter might provide intoxication, but in sufficient quantities the stuff also blinded or even killed. Their version of *all sorts*, one of their most popular drinks, consisted of whatever beverages patrons left on their tables—both mild and strong drink, tea, coffee, even milk and broth—all mixed together and ladled from a giant crock.

Frederick seemed none the worse for what he drank, and Annie figured that what filled his pail had to be at least half beer. "I'll give you a penny for half," Annie said, "then you can go get more."

"Yeah," Frederick said, "I'll go for that."

Annie fished a penny from her pocket and offered the coin to him. He gave her the pail, and she drained off half in a series of deep gulps.

"Mind you don't take too much," Frederick said.

She handed the pail back to him. He lifted the vessel, and drank the contents except for a small amount that dribbled from the left side of his mouth. Then he headed up the stairs, calling over his shoulder, "Be back in a trice."

Annie felt a moderate warming in her belly from the drink. As she waited, a gurgling sound in her breathing brought out fear of another coughing fit. Until then, she had forgotten about her medicine. She coughed into her hands and saw blood in her right palm.

Hearing footsteps again on the stairs leading down to the kitchen, she quickly wiped the gore on her black skirt. Something inside her—possibly the girl—wanted to keep the blood a secret.

Perhaps she believes that should I not think about the blood, and nobody else knows about it, then I am not ill.

Not Eliza or Frederick, but another lodger entered the kitchen—William Stevens, a short fair-haired fellow, a printer by trade. His clothing frequently displayed ink spatters.

"Hello, Dark Annie," he said. "I'm here for matches."

"Mr. Donovan hides them behind the lip of the shelves, there," she said, pointing to the other side of the room.

He fetched a small box from a recess at one end of a set of shelves built into the wall.

Though she'd tried, Annie couldn't forget the blood from her cough.

Thoughts of the disease, consumption, came to mind and she pushed them away. As long as she had something to help her cough, she would get better.

She got out her pill box. The crack along one side had widened. Even as she tried to open the box, the wood broke apart and three pills fell to the tabletop. She took one up, put the tablet in her mouth, and swallowed.

Seeing a piece of paper beside the fireplace, Annie got up and retrieved it. Part of a used envelope, it would do a good job holding her remaining pills.

"And how are you this fine evening," William asked.

"Better since I went to get money from my sister in Vauxhall."

"Good for you," he said.

Annie had hoped Frederick would come back with his pail of beer. She also waited for Eliza, and knew that her willingness to kill time for that purpose came with a diminished fear of the street. As miserable as sleeping rough had been, she'd survived the ordeal, and she knew she could again, if need be.

Even so, she would avoid the experience if possible. A little more, two pence, ha'penny, and she'd be able to go to a doss house. Perhaps she'd find a client to pay that much.

Enough waiting. Annie rose from the table and headed up the stairs. "Goodnight," she said.

He followed her up, "And to you," he said. William took the flight up to the second floor as Annie exited the building to make another round of the pubs.

Bonnet

"Have you been drinking, John?" Annie asked.

John had come in late, about ten o'clock in the evening, from attending his gentleman, a farm bailiff named Weeks.

"Yes, darling," he said. "I'd hoped you wouldn't notice. Not because I'm sorry I did. Because I didn't want to tempt you. I stopped with Stephen Trembley at the Yellow Dog and bought him a couple. He's stood in for me with Mr. Weeks a few times this month. I had but one small glass of whiskey."

Annie tried to put on a brave face. The odor on his breath brought strong memories of intoxication, many of them unpleasant, many of them exquisitely beautiful, such as meeting and falling in love with John himself. When they'd met, she'd already begun to establish some independence from her family, especially her mother, and had been feeling more as if her choices belonged to her alone. She'd been having more success at setting aside some of the sense of responsibility for her father's death. And, of course, John's attention, his loving gaze and caresses, his kind words and his encouragement of her new sense of self, had helped to form an exquisite bond with him she'd never suspected might exist between two human beings. Once caught up in that bond, she'd known that she'd craved his love all her life.

"I understand the need," she said.

Annie hoped her wistfulness didn't show. Since he'd collected her from Asherton House, John had said nothing to her about his expectations of her concerning drink. She suspected that he had not brought up the subject because he hadn't wanted her to suggest that he should also abstain. Annie didn't want to discuss the problem because she didn't want to be put in a position of having to promise never to drink again herself. If her resolve crumbled, the promise would come between them.

John shook his head. "Not need, love, merely desire."

Was he so different from her that he could set drink aside as needed? She knew that she could not. Once she started she always wanted more.

"I shall try harder to keep it away from you," he said.

And he did for the longest time. A month after Annie had joined John in Windsor she had settled into a comfortable, if solitary routine. She cooked and cleaned in the one-room cottage John rented from Mr. Weeks, and went to market for their food. Otherwise, she kept to herself, uncertain about being with others who might from time to time enjoy a drink. Thankfully, she wasn't thrust amongst others as she'd been in the tight confines of London. Those she saw on the streets looked at her with enough suspicion that she shied away.

Windsor had its beauties. She found planted fields and fields for grazing livestock, trees, hedge rows, even forest, all with an abundance of clean air. Despite a desire to explore, she had some small fear of the wilder aspects of the landscape. No doubt the land all belonged to someone, possibly even the queen, and Annie didn't want to run afoul of the law, accidentally trespassing or being mistaken for a poacher. She thought her inhibition laughable, and didn't speak to John about it.

She and John had been happier than at any time in recent memory. For Annie, that was in part because her children remained in London and she had little responsibility. Yet the children were to join them in Windsor within a month. Although she dreaded finding herself unable to send them to her mother, she told herself that she would become accustomed to having them around, and that, sober, she'd learn to love them properly.

Even with a severe cold in the weeks before they were to arrive, John talked of little else but the reunion and his plans for what they would eat the first few nights and the places in Windsor he would take the children on outings.

One week before they arrived, on a Saturday, he was to attend Mr. Weeks at an outdoor event on a cold evening. John made a mystery of doing something at the warm fireplace before going out. When he turned to kiss Annie before leaving, she got the powerful odor of whiskey on his breath. She recoiled, though the odor attracted her powerfully. Still sick, he'd heated whiskey to soothe his sore throat, quiet his cough, and fortify himself against the growing chill outside.

"I'm sorry, love," he said, noticing her reaction. "I shouldn't have kissed you after that."

Annie shook her head, and said, "I know you needed it."

"For my cold," he said.

Although she nodded her head, Annie decided that what he'd said wasn't true. Envy rose up in her as he exited the stone cottage.

If he could have an occasional tip, she could too.

~ ~ ~

Annie awoke in a hayloft, a taste of rotten fruit in her mouth. Beside her lay a sleeping man. Amidst the scattered hay, she saw empty wine bottles and a partial bottle of brandy.

How had she got there? With the thought that another segment of memory had gone missing, fear and self-loathing gripped her and churned in her gut. Annie rolled to one side and vomited in the loose hay. When done, she turned back to consider the sleeping man, and tried to recollect the chain of events that had put her there.

He snored loudly. His long face, curly auburn hair, and sharp nose tugged at her memory. His clothes—the plum-colored silk waistcoat and white linen shirt that remained on him, and the striped brown wool trousers, the fitted jacket, and the shoes strewn about the loft—suggested middle class. As Annie sat up, she felt a stiffness in the backside of her skirts.

She'd had sexual relations with the man! Her skirts were stiff with the dried fluid of his seed.

Fighting her hangover for control of her limbs, Annie crawled to the ladder and climbed down to ground level. She heard horses moving in the stalls to either side, and someone outside walking toward the stable. She crouched in shadows behind a broken down trap.

Mr. Weeks, John's employer entered. Short in stature and "broad in the beam," as Annie's mother might have said, his body could have belonged to a soft, plump woman, yet the small angry face in his large head became a frightful thing to look upon.

Annie crouched lower hoping he would not begin a search of the stable.

"Harry" he shouted. A spray of spittle, cast with the words, glinted in the early light slanting in through the doorway. "Where are you, you wretched ratbag layabout!"

Annie remembered a conversation with the man in the loft. They'd sat together in the Yellow Dog talking about John and Mr. Weeks. "Your John, he drove me away from my brother's property a fortnight ago when I come to ask for money."

The man in the loft was Mr. Weeks brother, Harold. John had pointed him out in the market one day. "He causes his brother no end of trouble with his drinking and gambling," John had said.

"I've seen him in here the worse for drink many times," Harry Weeks had said of John last night.

Annie had searched the cottage for John's whiskey without finding any. She walked a mile and a half to the Yellow Dog pub, taking the funds he had given her to buy their food.

No, I didn't do that, did I? That didn't happen.

She knew the events had taken place, as memories from the night before began to flow more freely. She'd been angry to think that John thought he could drink while he clearly thought she should not. At the pub, she sat drinking rum alone until Harry Weeks came in and approached her.

"You're new to these parts," he said, and she smiled.

Mr. Weeks climbed the ladder to the loft. "Harry!" he shouted again, once he'd got within view of his brother. "Wake up!"

The snores coming from above ceased, and Annie heard mumbling.

"You broke in last night to steal my wine."

"I didn't…" came the voice Annie remembered from the night before.

"Climb down or be thrown off," Mr. Weeks said.

Annie had to get out before they saw her. She moved toward the partially opened door, but tripped as she scrambled forward. Impact with the ground forced a soft cry from her.

"Stop her," Mr. Weeks said.

She got to her feet, glanced back to see him struggling to get past his brother who was starting down the ladder.

Her heart racing, head pounding with hangover pain, Annie ran. She stumbled again, this time losing her bonnet, the one she'd received at Asherton House.

Annie told herself that Harry would keep her name out of whatever he said to his brother. She would find a lie to give John to explain away her absence.

When she got to the stone cottage, to her relief, John wasn't home. He was to have the day off after attending his gentleman the night before. No doubt, he'd left to look for her.

Without anyone there to stoke the fire in the fireplace against the chill October air, the cottage had grown cold. Annie lifted an older bonnet from a hook beside the door to help keep the chill off. Placing it on her head, she remembered with horror that her name had been stitched with care by someone at the Asherton House asylum into the bonnet she'd dropped fleeing the angry Mr. Weeks.

Having embarrassed and cost John his job in the past, and likely having done so again, Annie knew she could not face her husband. Thinking of the children coming the following week and imagining what future harm she might do them, she panicked.

Annie found the household funds, amounting to about eight pounds. She took enough shillings to equal three pounds, packed a bag of clothes, and began walking toward the train station.

Twenty-Nine
Friday, September 7

By one o'clock in the morning, fearing that she probably wouldn't find a client in time to secure a bed, Annie decided she needed to fortify herself against the possibility that she faced another night on the streets. With the pence, ha'penny in her pocket, she bought a glass of bitter and a baked potato at the Cock and Hoop. She downed the bitter at the pub, returned her glass to the bar, then wandered back to Crossingham's with the continued hope of finding Eliza. Several layers of paper wrapped around the potato kept the food hot and protected Annie's hands from burns.

When she got to the lodging house, Mrs. Evans, the night watchman's wife, was going into the building. She knew the woman to be hard of hearing. Annie entered quietly right behind her, hoping the draft from the opening of the door a second time would not be noticed amidst the cool air that entered with Mrs. Evans. At that late hour, if Annie got to the kitchen, an hour might pass before Mr. Evans came in and found her.

Inside, she saw Mrs. Evans standing in the doorway to the deputy's office. Mr. Donovan's voice could be heard within. The woman blocked his view of the building's entrance. Annie slipped silently to the left toward the stairs. She'd got by unseen, but then her heart sank with the creaking of the stairs.

She'd not completely unwrapped her potato before Mr. Evans entered. "You've had quite enough of our hospitality without paying, Annie," he said. "I'll have to ask you to leave."

"Is my bed still available?" she asked, although she had no idea how she would pay.

"Number 29 is empty."

Annie took up her potato and wrapping, climbed the stairs, and entered Mr. Donovan's office.

"Dark Annie," he said.

"I haven't enough for my bed yet," she said. "Please don't let number 29. Won't be long before I'm in for the night." She had no confidence that what she said was true, and she could see that the deputy didn't either.

"I hear you had a drink earlier with Frederick Simons," Mr. Donovan said. "You find money for your beer, and none for your bed."

Annie didn't respond. He said nothing more for a time, and she stood for a while trying to think of something that would persuade him to allow her into the room without paying. Nothing she came up with seemed reasonable. Again, she almost said something about wanting to meet with Eliza, but held back for the same reason as before.

"Never you mind," Annie said, as if he had been listening to, and, like her, rejecting the arguments and suggestions she posed within her mind. "Soon, I shall be back. Please don't let number 29."

She passed Mr. Evans on her way out. "Won't be long before I'm back, Brummy. See that he saves my bed."

Not far along Dorset Street, Annie turned into Little Praternoster Row. She ate her potato and dropped its wrapper as she headed toward Brushfield street.

There's still a chance—one more round of the pubs.

~ ~ ~

With the bells for two o'clock in the morning, Annie had given up all hope of clients and beds, and turned her attention to looking for a spot to sleep rough. As she moved along Brick Lane, hurrying between the islands of gas lamp light, she remembered how vulnerable she felt after leaving John. She had feared most the possibility of having no place to sleep at night, that while insensible in slumber on the streets, she would dangerously expose herself to the malevolent forces that moved more freely in the darkness.

The three pounds she had taken from the household funds when she'd left John had carried Annie for a short time. She found inexpensive doss houses in the East End. She bought thread, yarn, and accoutrements for crocheting, knitting, lacemaking, and tatting. Using the skills she gained at the Asherton House asylum, she made products to sell on the street so she wouldn't have to beg.

From the Commercial Street Post Office, she wrote to John expressing her regrets, apologizing for the harm she'd inflicted upon him and the children, and saying that she was done ruining their lives.

"I know you will all get on just fine if you don't have to pick up after my drunken ways," she wrote.

John sent back a letter.

Dearest Annie,
Your children need you and I need you. They are with your mother still. I send her money for their care. I shall send you 10 shillings each week until you return. I love you darling and always will.
John

In the envelope with his letter, she found a post office order for ten shillings.

From her family, she later learned that he lost his valet position with Mr. Weeks, and that he then found work again as a coachman.

The children had remained with Mum.

Annie had not loved any of the men she'd taken up with since. They'd been merely a means to lighten the load on her meager income. The compromises she made to her dignity had increased with each new relationship.

John sent the ten shillings in the same manner each week until he died. He also sent funds to Mum to help her with the children.

Annie didn't like to think that she'd left John and the children so she'd have the freedom to drink.

Who would suffer such poverty for that?

She looked to those times when she did without drink as proof that she still had the ability to defy the want, yet most often a lack of funds had driven the decision to abstain. Still, that lack of funds had indeed prevented her from sinking as deep in the lush as she'd got while with John. In recent years, Annie had avoided the state in which she became willing to harm others to pursue her need.

Well, that is, until she saw Eliza palming the florin. Though different from mistreating and abandoning her children and costing her husband his livelihood, she knew that the desperation that drove such unthinking and deceptive behavior was much the same.

The dishonesty that comes with the drink hurts more than any hangover.

Annie knew from what she gathered from family that John drank himself into an early grave. He died alone on Christmas day in 1886.

How can he smile upon me the way he does?

Annie didn't think she deserved such devotion. She had cried about the loss of the man enough. Turning again to the one thing within her power to help her feel better about herself, she thought, *Tomorrow, I shall find Eliza, confess my true purpose in chaunting her theft, apologize, and beg for mercy.* She laughed uneasily. *Hopefully, she won't nobble me again.*

More than just the right thing to do for Eliza, expressing her regret to the woman would make a positive difference in Annie's sense of herself.

I will have no more to do with the likes of Eddie. I shall earn my bed and board by honest means from now on.

~ ~ ~

Annie tried to remember where she'd been when she met the constable who gave her fifteen minute intervals of sleep on Wednesday night/Thursday morning. If she could find his beat, she might get some rest. Memory served only endless brick walls and paving stones illuminated by gas lamp; nothing that stood out as a landmark.

Like the constable had suggested, she chose a shadowed space where the gas lamp light didn't reach. She rested beside a tool house attached to an old wooden home. To stay out of the light, she crouched with her legs pulled in tight. A constable found her before she dozed off.

Although thin for a bed and a bit high—about eight feet off the ground—she tried to rest on the stout horizontal beam of wooden bracing between two sagging brick buildings. She tucked her skirts under her legs to keep them from falling below the beam and enlarging her silhouette. Fearing that she might fall in her sleep, she dozed fitfully, flinching awake several times as she imagined striking the pavers beneath.

Annie did not know how long she might have slept when she felt a tugging on her skirts. No doubt they'd come loose and fallen as she shifted in sleep. She'd been caught again.

Annie tried a couple more spots with no success. Finally, as she had done Wednesday night/Thursday morning, she joined the countless homeless persons shambling along the streets. Again, she found herself making a circuit that depended on Whitechapel Road and Hanbury Street as its east/west segments and a variety of roads for the north/south segments. Unlike her experience two nights earlier, her orbit and that of most of the homeless if seen from above would have shown a counter-clockwise course.

Remembering her notion from Wednesday night/Thursday morning that each completed orbit run clockwise represented a year of her life, Annie thought, *I now unwind time.*

The loose group she fell in with included numerous raggedy men, women, and children. They moved at different paces, and came and went from her view.

A brief period of full wakefulness occurred as a fellow, wheeling a barrow rapidly, veered toward her along Whitechapel Road. Startled, she cowered against the nearest building, imagining that he was the cat's meat man, finally come for her. Whatever he carried in the oilcloth sack in his barrow had a more powerful stench of death and decay than anything Annie had ever smelled.

Correcting his course, he went by without seeming to notice her. A tall, thin fellow with dark hair poking out from under his hat, he didn't look at all like the cat's meat man from her childhood. She paused to catch her breath, and nearly lost the potato in her stomach.

With time, as on Wednesday night, Annie found herself consistently walking with the same people, and encountered fewer traveling in the opposite direction. She saw a woman with four children ahead, and a tall older man beyond her. She glimpsed a younger man following behind, heard his tread.

Could they all be her trudging companions from Wednesday night/Thursday morning? That seemed unlikely. Annie had seen the woman's face. *I would recognize her*, she thought, yet couldn't gather the energy to call out or catch up with her and find out.

A light rain began to fall, reducing the figures to mere silhouettes and muffling sound. She hoped the downfall ceased before she became soaked through.

The woman ahead had the right number of children to be Annie's mother, and she followed the older man unerringly into the gloom, much the way Mum had done with Dadda.

Annie read the number, twenty-nine, painted on the brick building along Hanbury street that had the cat's meat sign in the window, and had the impression that she'd somehow walked to Brompton and passed by her mother's room at 29 Monpelier Place. The number had come to represent refuge, while the sign inspired dread.

The rain ceased. Annie heard the footsteps of the younger man following behind, and thought again of the cat's meat man. The sound didn't become louder. A brief glance back assured her that he didn't draw near. Something about his gait reminded her of John's.

Her feet had grown swollen and painful in her too-tight boots. The grind of her hips, knees, and ankles produced a dull agony, deep in the joints. Her eyes swelled in their sockets, putting an uncomfortable pressure on her brain. The potato in her stomach felt like a load of rocks. That hard kernel of something dreadful and weighty she'd found in her chest on Wednesday night/Thursday morning began to grow once more.

And again, Annie didn't have the presence of mind to find a way out of the odd, slow torture of her aimless trek. Obstinate time would not pass more swiftly.

The girl in Annie tried to provide escape in fancy—she decided that the old man in the lead was indeed her father, the woman and her four children were her mother and siblings, the man following behind was John, and each circuit in their orbit unwound a year of her life.

She got the idea that if she took a turn off the circuit at the right moment, she might take up there with her life, make different choices, and avoid some of the hardships she'd endured. If she chose well, perhaps her father might not kill himself, and she would understand the dangers of drink earlier in life.

But which turn to take in which circuit? *Should I take the wrong one, I might make things worse. I could lose John.* If she went back far enough to save Dadda, before she knew anything of John, she might miss meeting him. She hadn't kept track of how many times she'd been around the circuit. She'd met John relatively late in life. In her state of exhaustion, math had become impossible.

Distress over the choice of where to turn off her path grew into an ache in her head. Her thoughts remained too muddled to offer suggestions. Still, Annie knew she had to make a choice for the pain to end.

Approaching the building with the number twenty-nine on the front, she saw the older man disappear into the gloom ahead, while the woman and four children passed through a door leading into the structure.

This must be the year Dadda died and we removed to 29 Montpelier

Place.

She hesitated, wanting to follow her father, express her regrets, and somehow save him.

Annie glimpsed the cat's meat sign in the window, and got another fright. She turned and looked back.

John had caught up! He was a mere thirty feet away, his face hidden in the shadows beneath the brim of his hat. Although different circumstances from when they'd met at the Frizzin and Flint, Annie knew she must gather him into her mother's lodgings before she missed her chance. His feet moved quickly. *He* saw the urgency too.

Annie stopped and opened the door. He passed through and then she entered.

Excited to have him back, she followed the sound of his tread along a lightless hall. She bumped into him in the dark, held onto his coat tail for guidance. He smelled strange. *Where has he been?*

Annie heard fumbling in the dark. A door opened. She felt a cool breeze on her face. He moved forward and she followed, and they exited through the back of the building.

Annie didn't recognize the yard—all mud and stone. On her right, a small roof over stairs leading down to a cellar sat against the building.

John turned toward her.

What is he wearing? His clothing didn't fit him quite right.

As his head tilted back, the scant light reached under the brim of his hat.

Not John—the cat's meat man!

Annie stepped back toward the cellar stairs, felt with her left foot the drop-off, and bumped into the upright that supported the small roof. "No," she said, a scream ready behind the word as she tried to regain firm footing.

The cat's meat man gripped Annie's neck and bore down on her throat before she could get the louder sound out.

How!

He pulled her away from the stairs. The reflections in his dark eyes had the sharpness of teeth. His gaze bore in on hers, devouring her terror.

Time slowed as Annie clawed at him. His long arms held her away, kept her from reaching his head and face. She tore at his sides. His tough coat resisted her fingers. She kicked at the cat's meat man and raised her knees against him weakly, even as he bore her to the ground.

Stop! Annie thought, *before it's too late. I still have to make apologies!* Stillness.

The cat's meat man had become her father. *I left so life would be better for you,* he said. *I could not keep hurting the child, the girl. She continues to suffer. You must let go to save her.*

No, Annie thought, *I must fight.*

She tried to cough to clear her throat so she could speak. The passage didn't open. She tasted blood.

"The girl is all you have," John said. He held her in loving arms.

Dadda was gone.

The girl Annie had been stood behind John. Annie could not focus on her.

"Don't let her die alone," John said. "Don't let her stay. Take her with you and go, now."

But I… I thought you wanted me to live for her sake.

"No," he said, "the contrary. The hardship of your life is killing her. You're ill, and have no means."

Consumption.

"Yes," he said. "You might have lived longer. You would have been dead inside without her."

Distantly, Annie felt her throat collapse with a small pain. Darkness closed in on her.

"It's done, now," John said. "Your blood chilled to think of the girl as a ghost of wistfulness. She will become that if she remains. Should you linger, though you'll be dead, you will continue as a feeble spirit of sleepless hunger."

Continue? Annie thought of the slow, pointless agony of walking the East End as she'd done that week, doing so forevermore, unable to rest.

Does he mean I'm already dead?

She could no longer feel her limbs.

Go where?

"Does it matter?"

Although Annie had seen no real purpose in her life for some time, she'd met the struggle to survive with vigor. The mere thought of letting go felt uncomfortable until John put her right hand into one belonging to the girl. The child smiled, the expression so buoyant that it lifted into the air. Annie felt it alight on her own face and settle in with all the warmth and promise of her early life.

John placed a kiss on her forehead, much like the ones Dadda had given before bedtime when she was very young and he was still a happy man.

Nearly devoid of life, the miserable, muddy yard of 29 Hanbury Street had gone quiet.

Annie had been a tender child once.

In her last moments, she knew that something of her always would be.

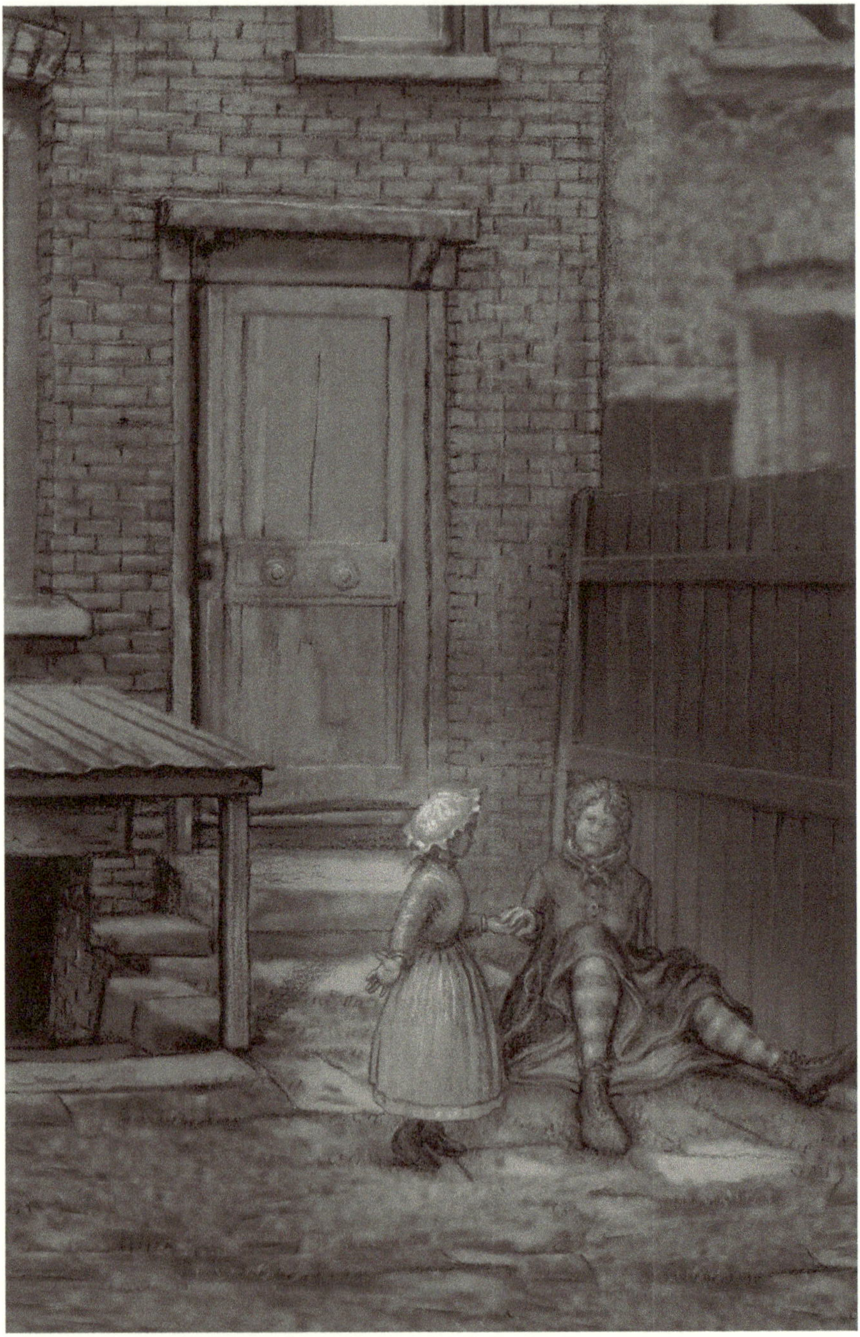

About the Author

Alan M. Clark, fine arts painter, illustrator, and author, hails from Tennessee where he grew up in a house full of human bones and old medical books. At present, he lives in Eugene, Oregon with his wife, Melody. In his 32 year freelance career, he has created illustrations for hundreds of books, including works of fiction of various genres, nonfiction, textbooks, young adult fiction, and children's books. He is the author of seventeen books, including eleven novels, a lavishly illustrated novella, four collections of fiction, and a nonfiction full-color book of his artwork. The World Fantasy Award and four Chesley Awards are among the honors he's received for his work. Mr. Clark's company, IFD Publishing, has released 37 books, including hardcovers, paperbacks, ebooks, and audio books. IFD Publishing's authors include F. Paul Wilson, Elizabeth Engstrom, and Jeremy Robert Johnson. www.alanmclark.com

Connect with the Author Online

You can email the author or find out more about him through the following websites:

http://www.ifdpublishing.com
http://www.smashwords.com/profile/view/IFDPublishing

IFD Publishing Paperbacks

Novels:
Of Thimble and Threat, by Alan M. Clark
Baggage Check, by Elizabeth Engstrom
Bull's Labyrinth, by Eric Witchey
The Surgeon's Mate: A Dismemoir, by Alan M. Clark
Siren Promised, by Jeremy Robert Johnson and Alan M. Clark
Say Anything but Your Prayers, by Alan M. Clark
Candyland, by Elizabeth Engstrom
Apologies to the Cat's Meat Man, by Alan M. Clark
Lizzie Borden, by Elizabeth Engstrom
A Parliament of Crows, by Alan M. Clark
Lizard Wine, by Elizabeth Engstrom
The Door that Faced West, by Alan M. Clark
The Northwoods Chronicles, by Elizabeth Engstrom
The Prostitute's Price, by Alan M. Clark
The Assassin's Coin, by John Linwood Grant
13 Miller's Court, by Alan M. Clark and John Linwood Grant
Guys Named Bob, by Elizabeth Engstrom

Collections:
Professor Witchey's Miracle Mood Cure, by Eric Witchey

Nonfiction:
How to Write a Sizzling Sex Scene, by Elizabeth Engstrom

IFD Publishing EBooks

(You can find the following titles at most distribution points for all ereading platforms.)

Novels:
The Prostitute's Price, by Alan M. Clark
The Assassin's Coin, by John Linwood Grant
13 Miller's Court, by Alan M. Clark and John Linwood Grant
Guys Named Bob, by Elizabeth Engstrom
Apologies to the Cat's Meat Man, by Alan M. Clark
Bull's Labyrinth, by Eric Witchey
The Surgeon's Mate: A Dismemoir, by Alan M. Clark
York's Moon, by Elizabeth Engstrom

Beyond the Serpent's Heart, by Eric Witchey
Lizzie Borden, by Elizabeth Engstrom
A Parliament of Crows, by Alan M. Clark
Lizard Wine, by Elizabeth Engstrom
Northwoods Chronicles, by Elizabeth Engstrom
Siren Promised, by Alan M. Clark and Jeremy Robert Johnson
To Kill a Common Loon, by Mitch Luckett
The Man in the Loon, by Mitch Luckett
Jack the Ripper Victim Series: Of Thimble and Threat by Alan M. Clark
Jack the Ripper Victim Series: The Double Event (includes two novels from the series: *Of Thimble and Threat* and *Say Anything But Your Prayers*) by Alan M. Clark
Candyland, by Elizabeth Engstrom
The Blood of Father Time: Book 1, The New Cut, by Alan M. Clark, Stephen C. Merritt & Lorelei Shannon
The Blood of Father Time: Book 2, The Mystic Clan's Grand Plot, by Alan M. Clark, Stephen C. Merritt & Lorelei Shannon
How I Met My Alien Bitch Lover: Book 1 from the Sunny World Inquisition Daily Letter Archives, by Eric Witchey
Baggage Check, by Elizabeth Engstrom
D. D. Murphry, Secret Policeman, by Alan M. Clark and Elizabeth Massie
Black Leather, by Elizabeth Engstrom

Novelettes:
The Tao of Flynn, by Eric Witchey
To Build a Boat, Listen to Trees, by Eric Witchey

Children's Illustrated:
The Christmas Thingy, by F. Paul Wilson. Illustrated by Alan M. Clark

Collections:
Suspicions, by Elizabeth Engstrom
Professor Witchey's Miracle Mood Cure, by Eric Witchey

Short Fiction:
"Brittle Bones and Old Rope," by Alan M. Clark
"Crosley," by Elizabeth Engstrom
"The Apple Sniper," by Eric Witchey

Nonfiction:
How to Write a Sizzling Sex Scene, by Elizabeth Engstrom
Divorce by Grand Canyon, by Elizabeth Engstrom

IFD Publishing Audio Books

Novels:
The Door That Faced West by Alan M. Clark, read by Charles Hinckley
Jack the Ripper Victim Series: Of Thimble and Threat, by Alan M. Clark, read by Alicia Rose
Jack the Ripper Victim Series: Say Anything But Your Prayers, by Alan M. Clark, read by Alicia Rose
Jack the Ripper Victim Series: The Double Event by Alan M. Clark, read by Alicia Rose (includes two novels from the series: *Of Thimble and Threat* and *Say Anything But Your Prayers*)
A Parliament of Crows by Alan M. Clark, read by Laura Jennings
A Brutal Chill in August by Alan M. Clark, read by Alicia Rose
The Surgeon's Mate: A Dismemoir, by Alan M. Clark, read by Alan M. Clark
Apologies to the Cat's Meat Man, by Alan M. Clark, read by Alicia Rose
The Prostitute's Price, by Alan M. Clark, read by Alicia Rose
The Assassin's Coin, by John Linwood Grant, read by Alicia Rose
13 Miller's Court, by Alan M. Clark and John Linwood Grant, read by Alicia Rose

Milton Keynes UK
Ingram Content Group UK Ltd.
UKHW021550050824
1158UKWH00013B/33